CLASSICS FROM
The Silver Screen

Arranged for Easy Piano by
JOHN BRIMHALL

Project Manager: TONY ESPOSITO
Production Coordinator: HANK FIELDS
Art Layout: LISA GREENE MANE

© 2000 WARNER BROS. PUBLICATIONS
All Rights Reserved

Any duplication, adaptation or arrangement of the compositions
contained in this collection requires the written consent of the Publisher.
No part of this book may be photocopied or reproduced in any way without permission.
Unauthorized uses are an infringement of the U.S. Copyright Act and are punishable by law.

CONTENTS

All the Way 6

As Time Goes By 8

Can You Read My Mind? 10

Dear Heart 12

Emily 14

Evergreen 16

I Will Wait for You 3

Laura 26

Little Boy Lost 23

Love Is a Many-Splendored Thing 28

Over the Rainbow 30

Secret Love 33

The Shadow of Your Smile 36

Somewhere My Love 38

The Summer Knows 46

Theme From Ice Castles (Through the Eyes of Love) 20

Three Coins in the Fountain 40

Whatever Will Be, Will Be (Que Sera, Sera) 42

Young at Heart 44

I WILL WAIT FOR YOU

Arranged by
JOHN BRIMHALL

English Words by NORMAN GIMBEL
Music by MICHEL LEGRAND

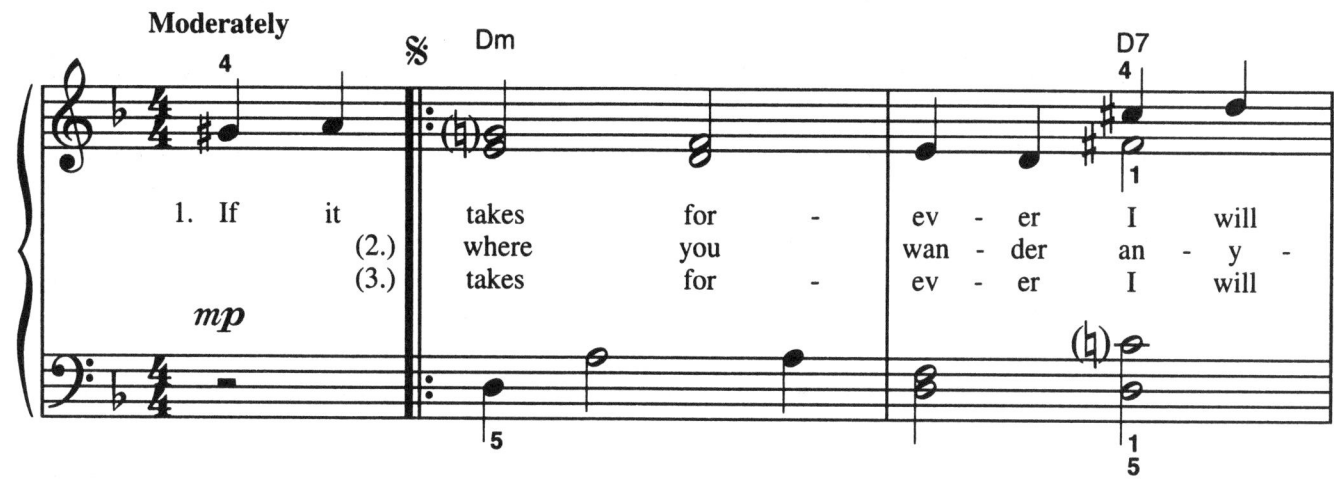

© 1965 PRODUCTIONS MICHEL LEGRAND and PRODUCTIONS FRANCIS LEMARQUE
© 1964, 1974 SONGS OF POLYGRAM INTERNATIONAL, INC. and JONWARE MUSIC CORP.
Copyrights Renewed
All Rights Reserved   Used by Permission

Dm
D7
Gm
back be - side me, 'til I'm hold - ing
heart be - lieve what in my heart I
back be - side me, 'til I'm touch - ing
Em7(♭5)
Dm/A
Em7
A7
you 'til I hear you sigh here in my
know that for - ev - er more I'll wait for
you and for - ev - er more shar - ing your
1.
Dm
Gm7
A7
arms.
2. An - y -
2.
Dm
Gm6
you.
Dm
To Interlude
The
3.
Dm
Gm6
Dm
Fine
love.
rit.
p

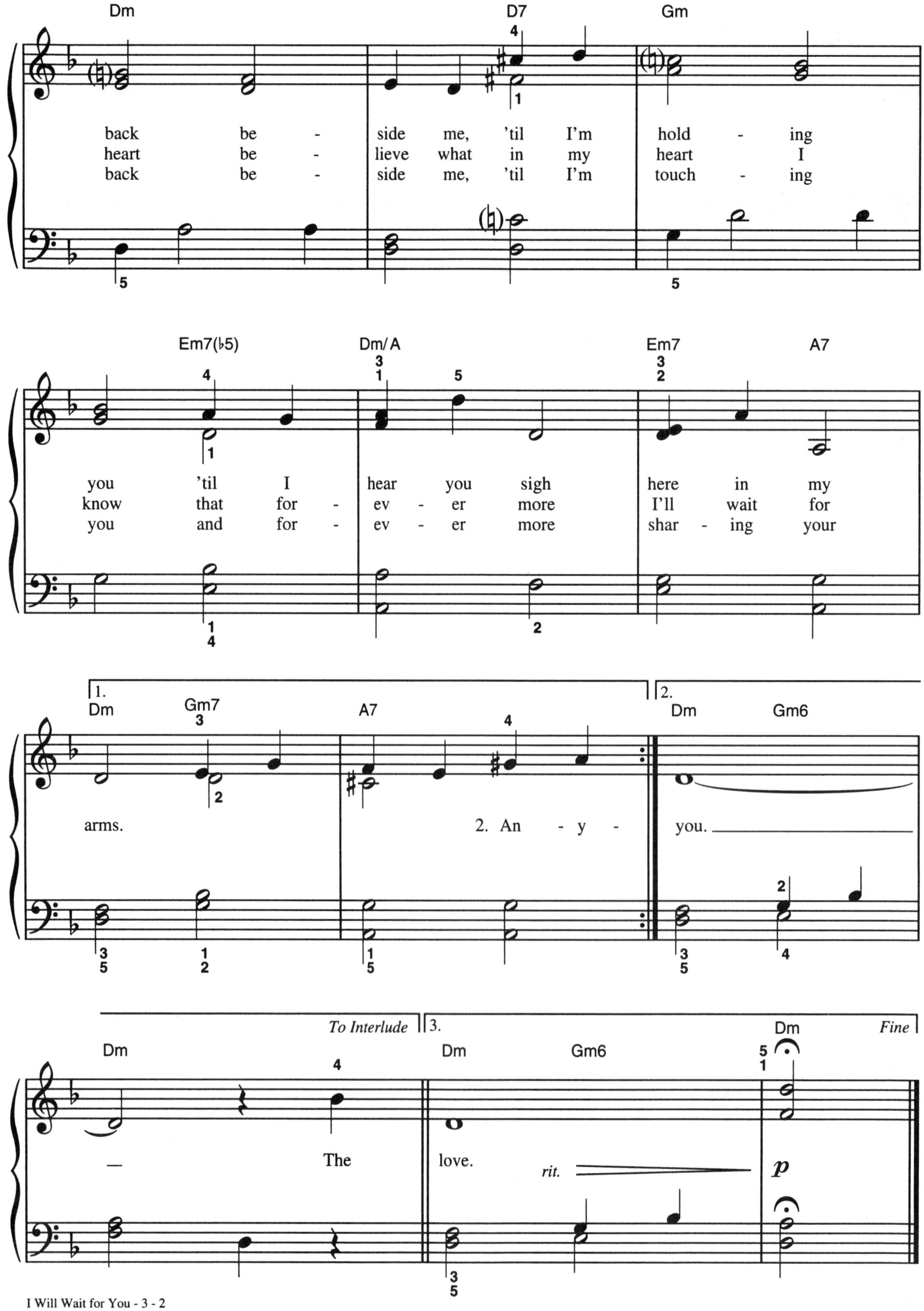

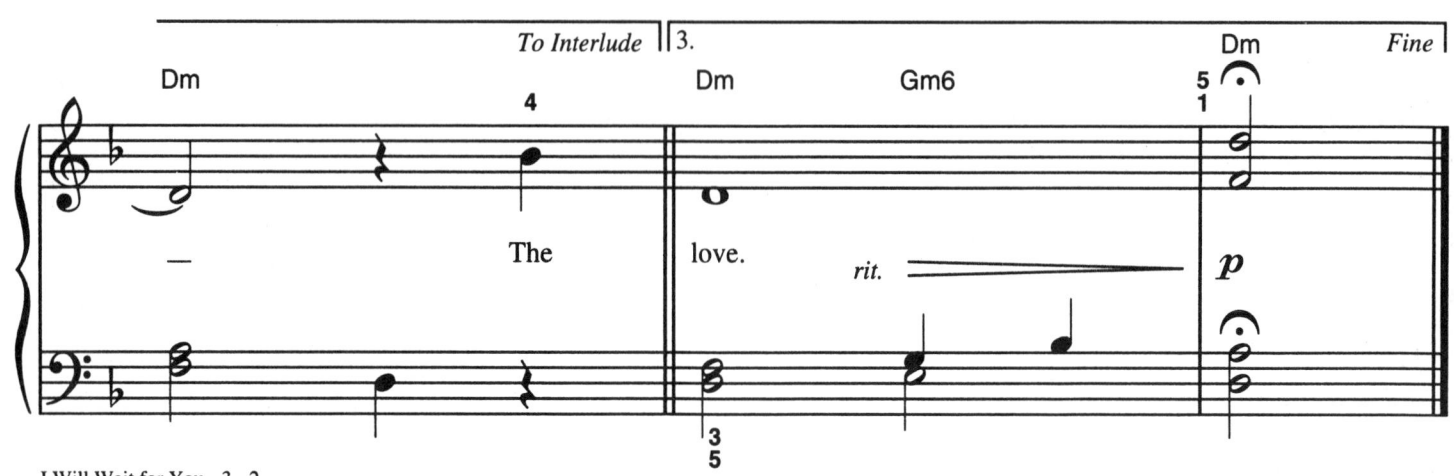

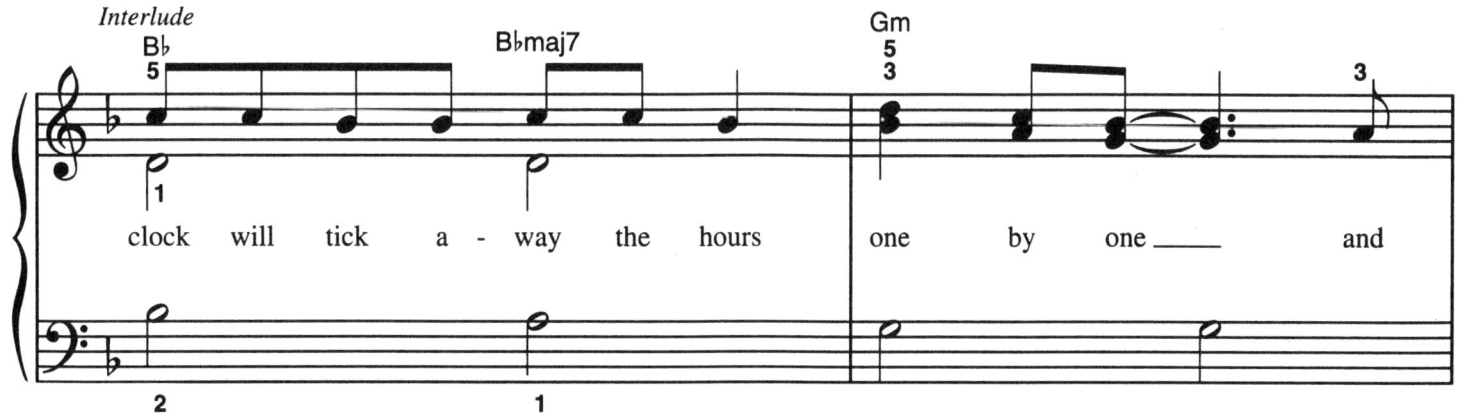

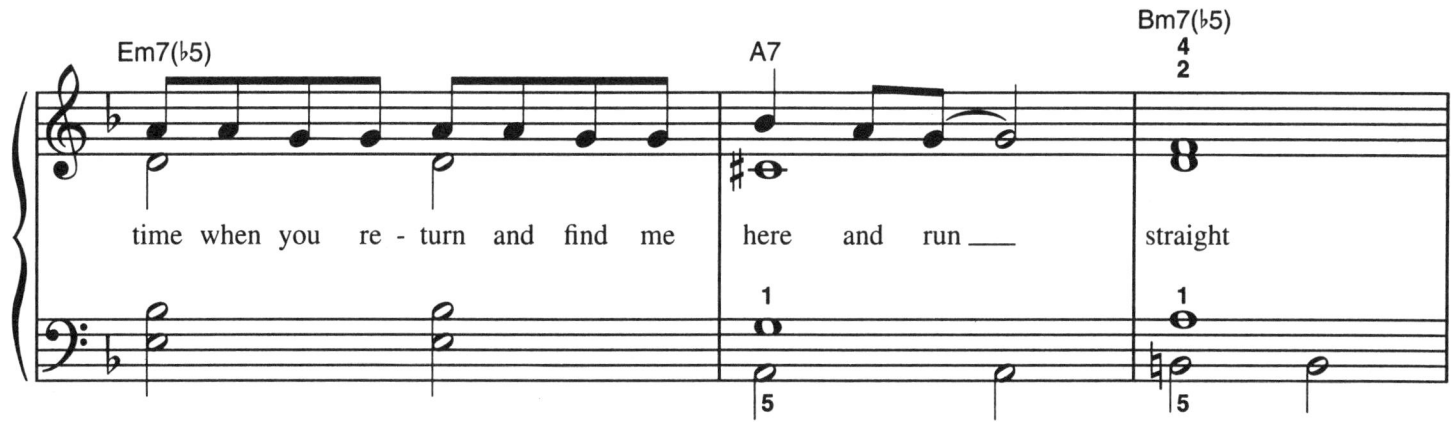
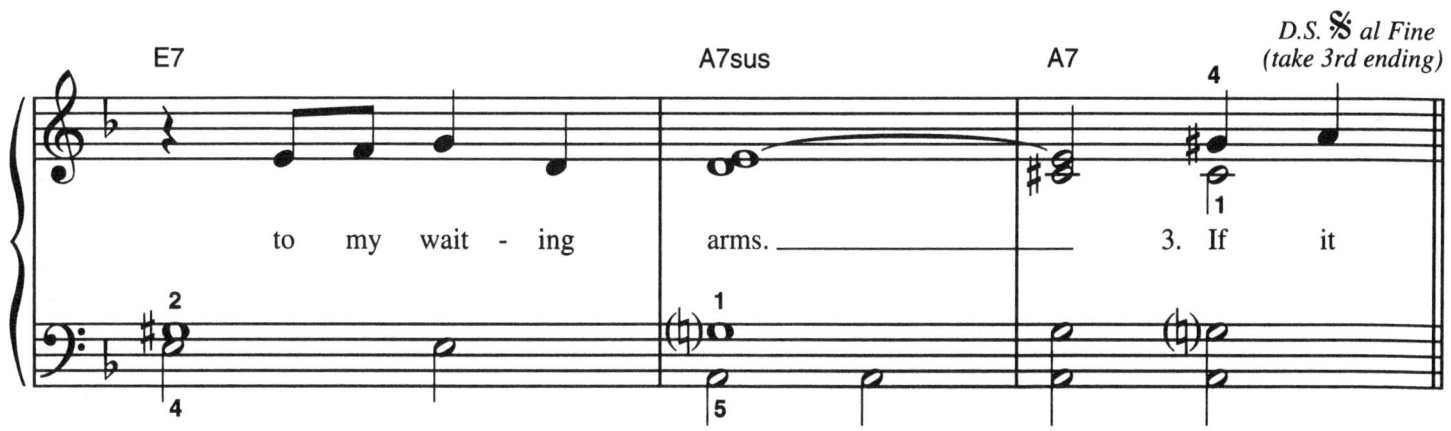

ALL THE WAY

Arranged by JOHN BRIMHALL

Lyrics by SAMMY CAHN
Music by JAMES VAN HEUSEN

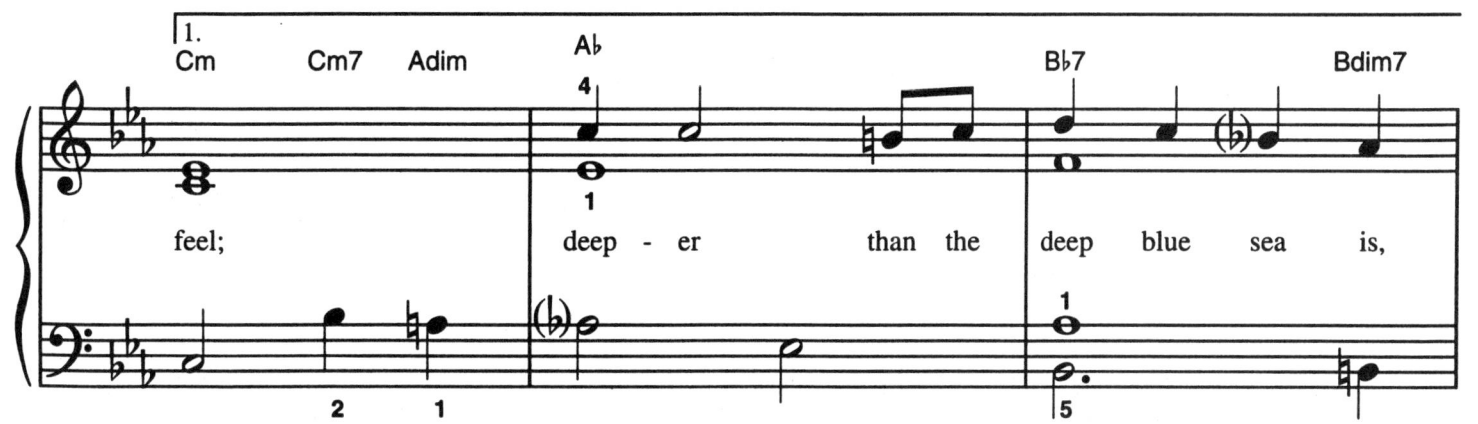
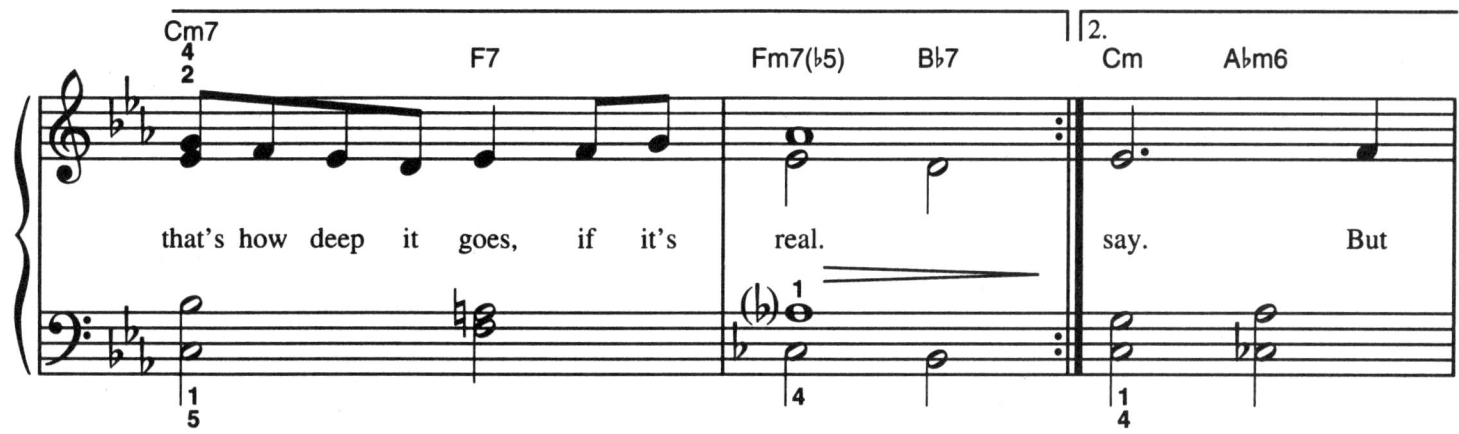

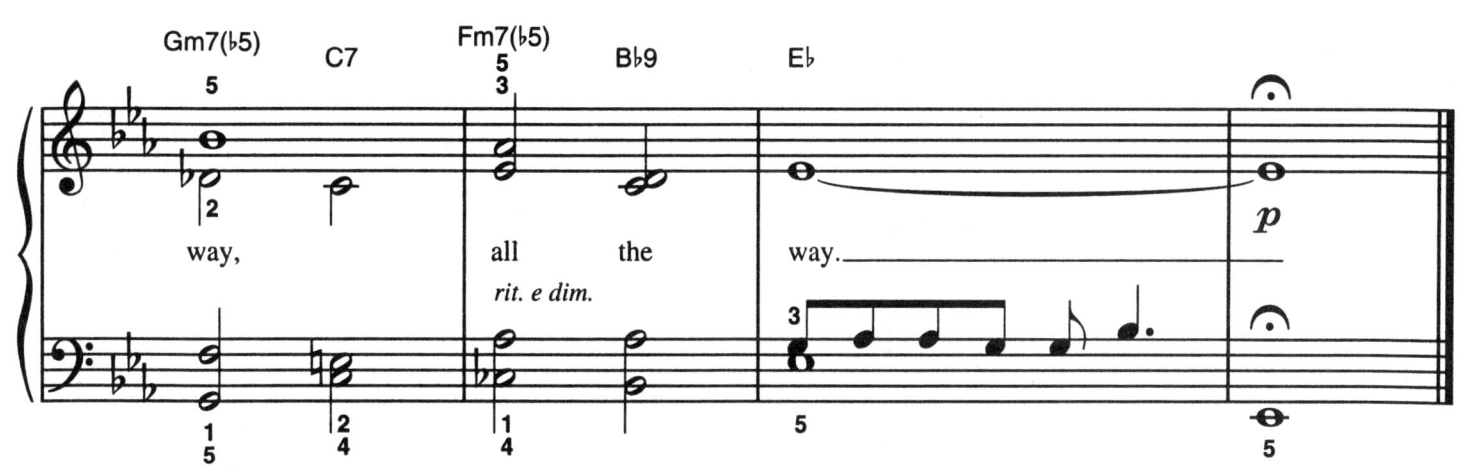

AS TIME GOES BY

Arranged by
JOHN BRIMHALL

Words and Music by
HERMAN HUPFELD

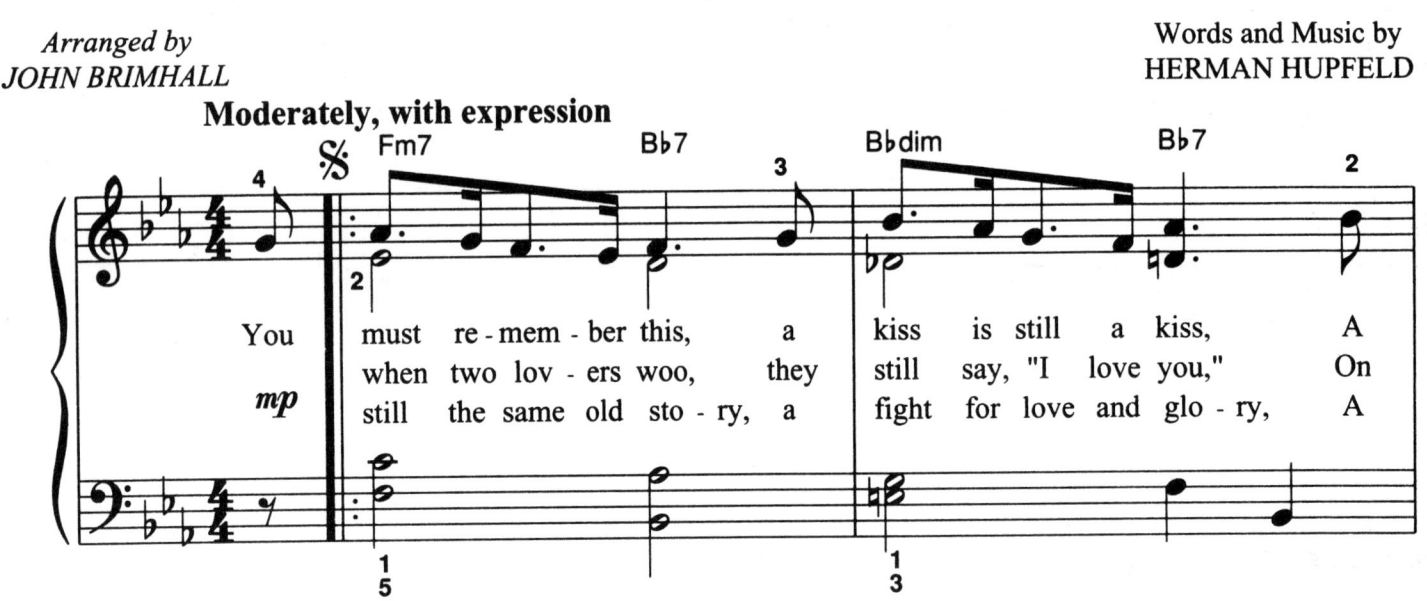

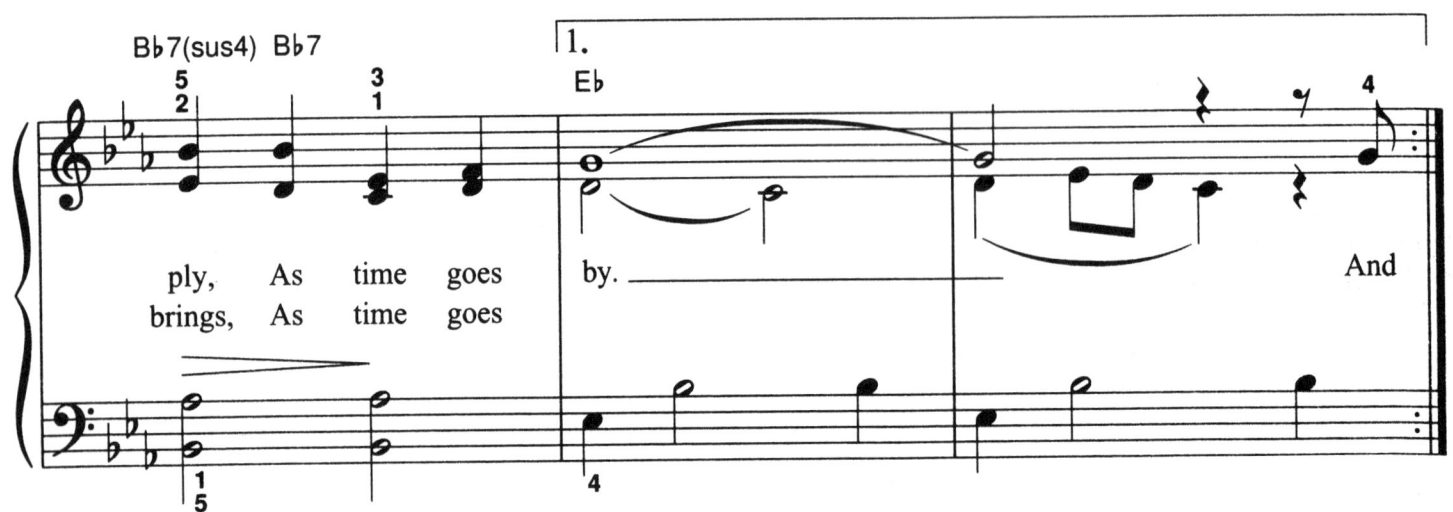

© 1931 WARNER BROS. INC. (Renewed)
This Arrangement © 1995 WARNER BROS. INC.
All Rights Reserved

CAN YOU READ MY MIND?
(Love Theme from "SUPERMAN")

Arranged by
JOHN BRIMHALL

Words by LESLIE BRICUSSE
Music by JOHN WILLIAMS

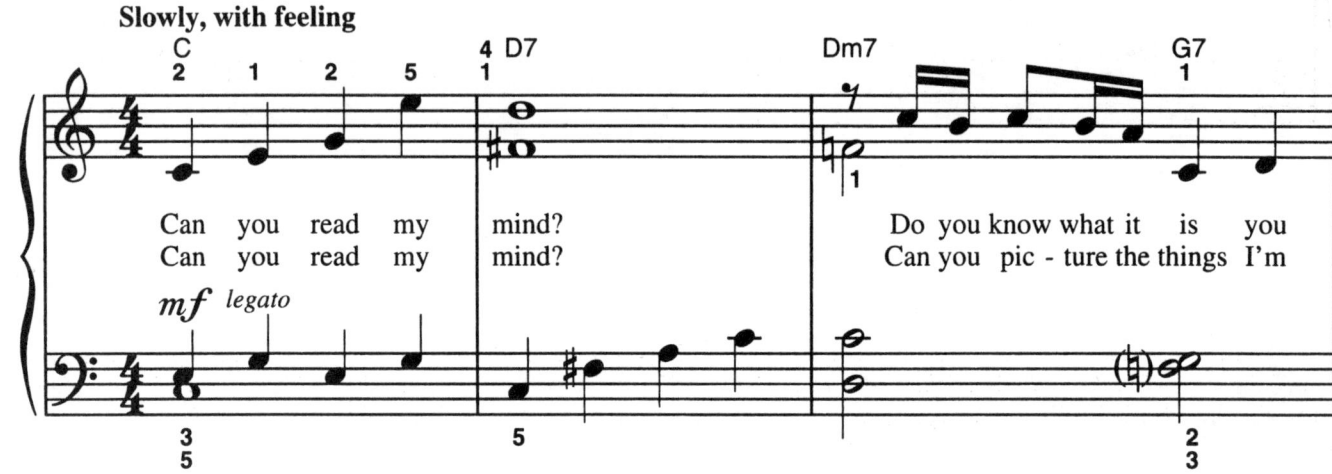

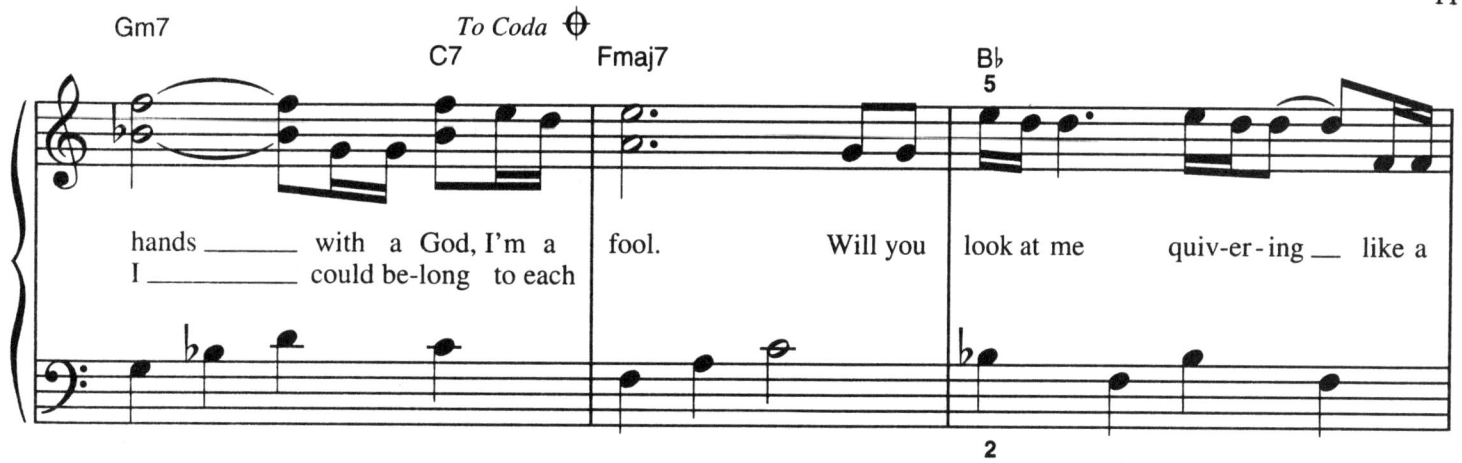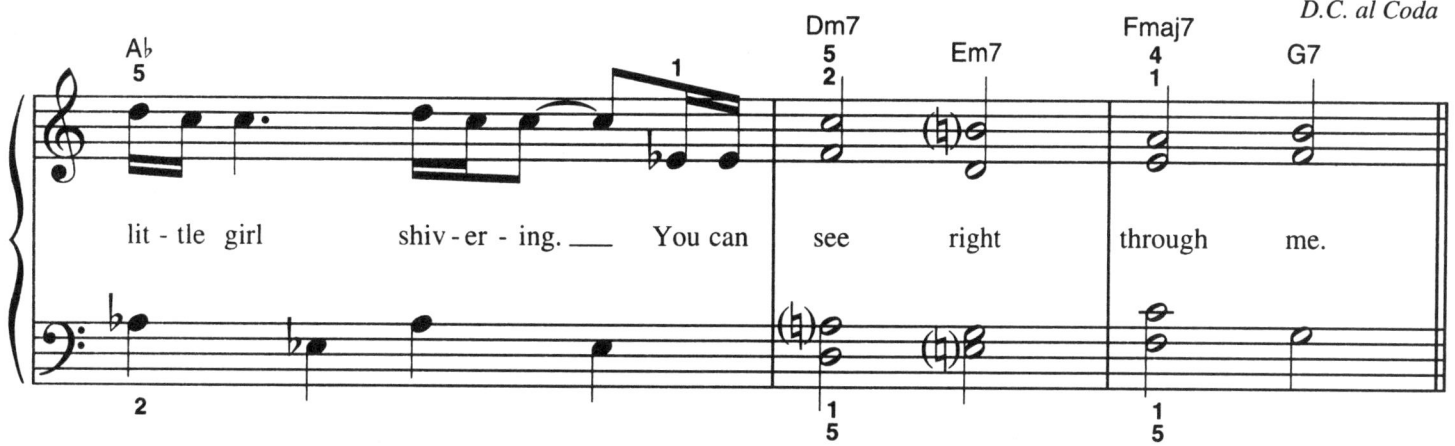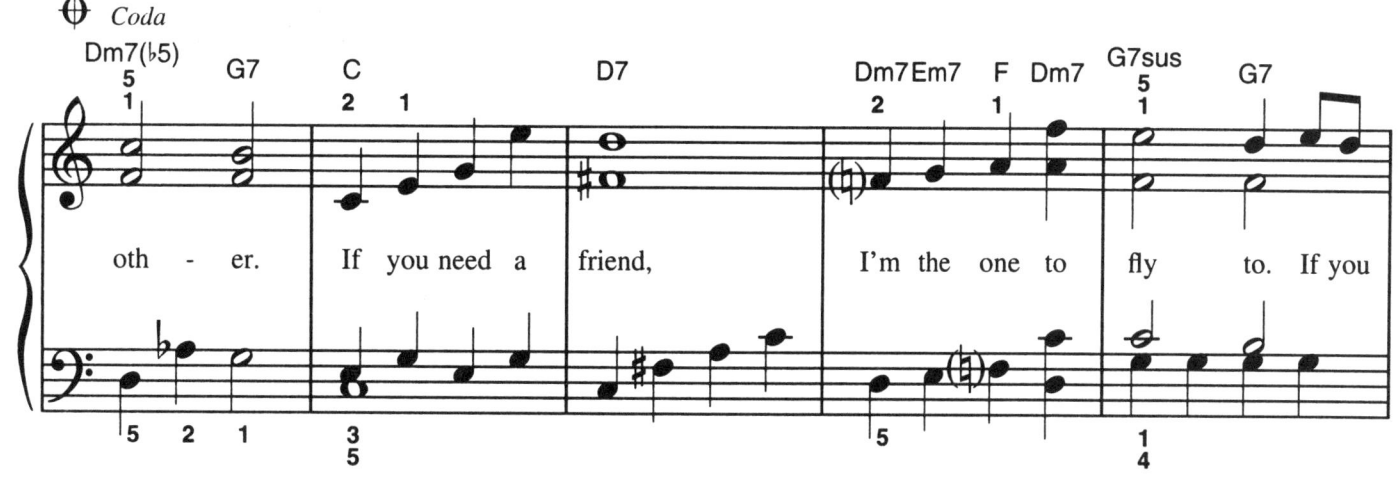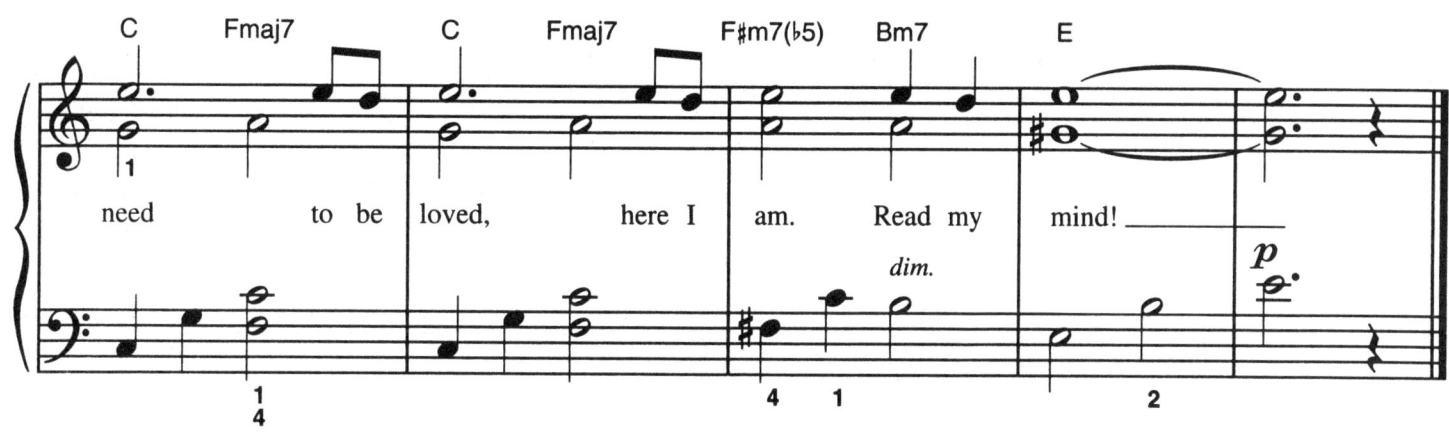

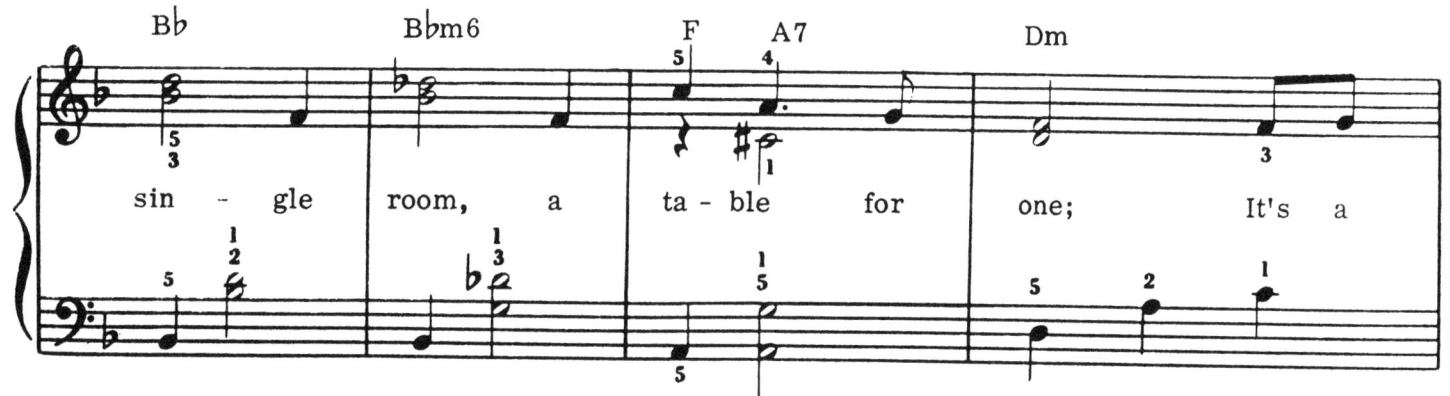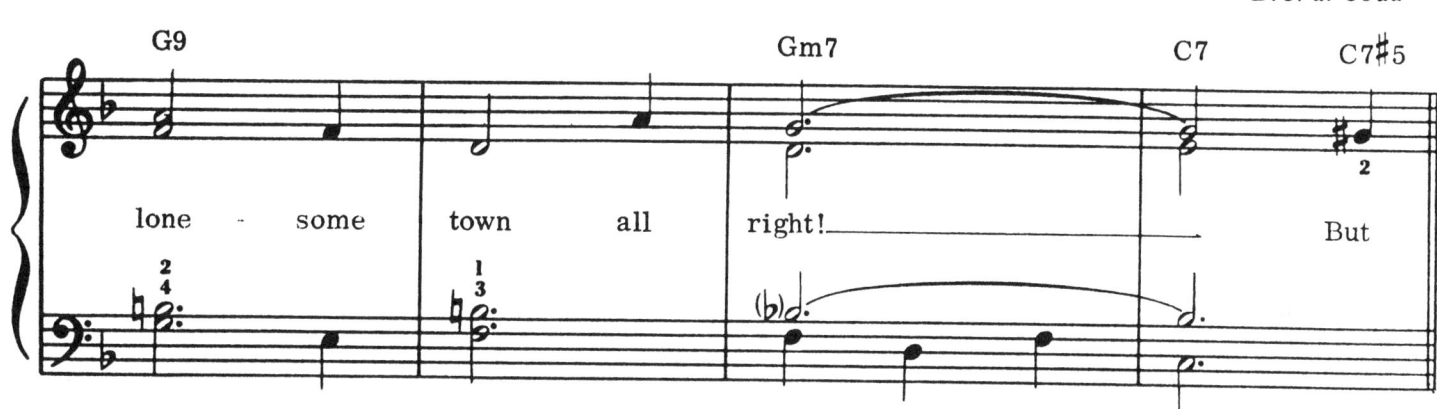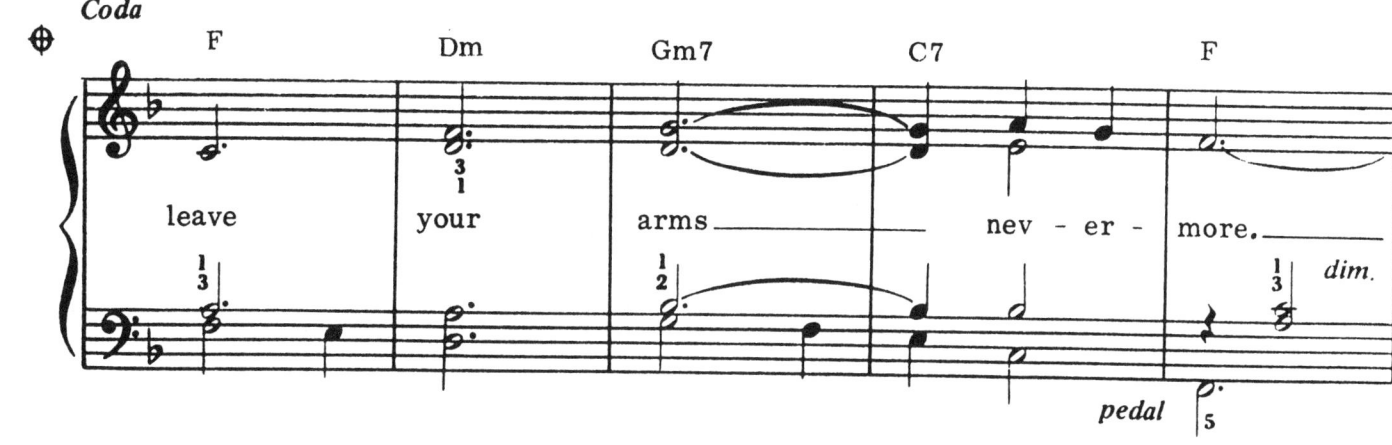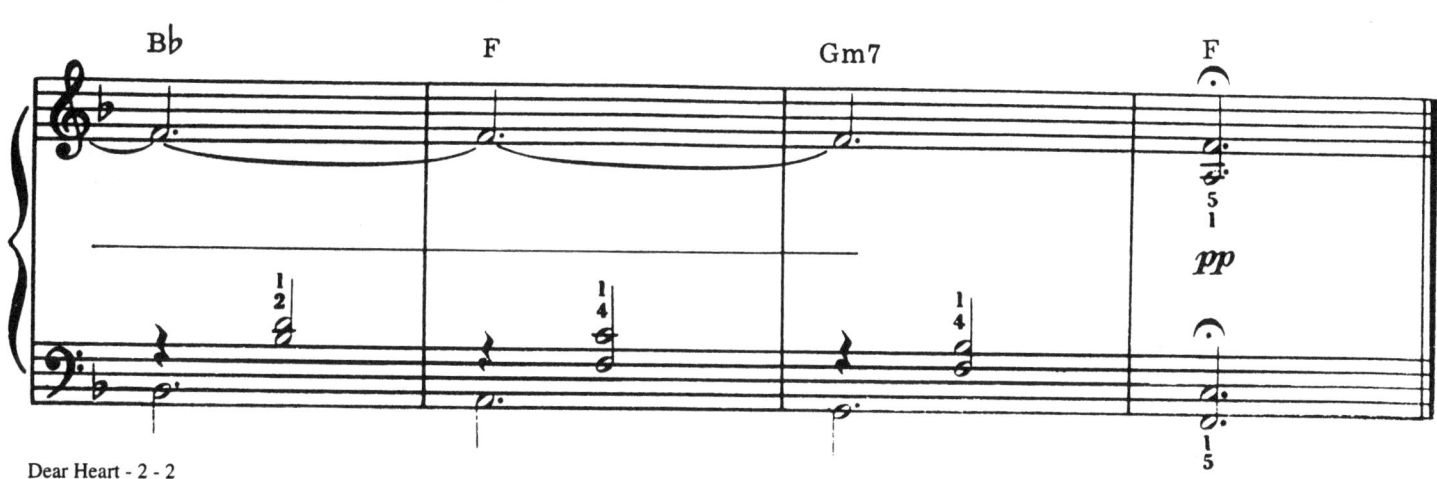

EMILY

Arranged by
JOHN BRIMHALL

By
JOHNNY MERCER and JOHNNY MANDEL

EVERGREEN

Arranged by
JOHN BRIMHALL

Words by PAUL WILLIAMS
Music by BARBRA STREISAND

Evergreen - 4 - 1

© 1976 FIRST ARTISTS MUSIC CO., EMANUEL MUSIC CORP. & WB MUSIC CORP.
All Rights Administered by WB MUSIC CORP.
All Rights Reserved

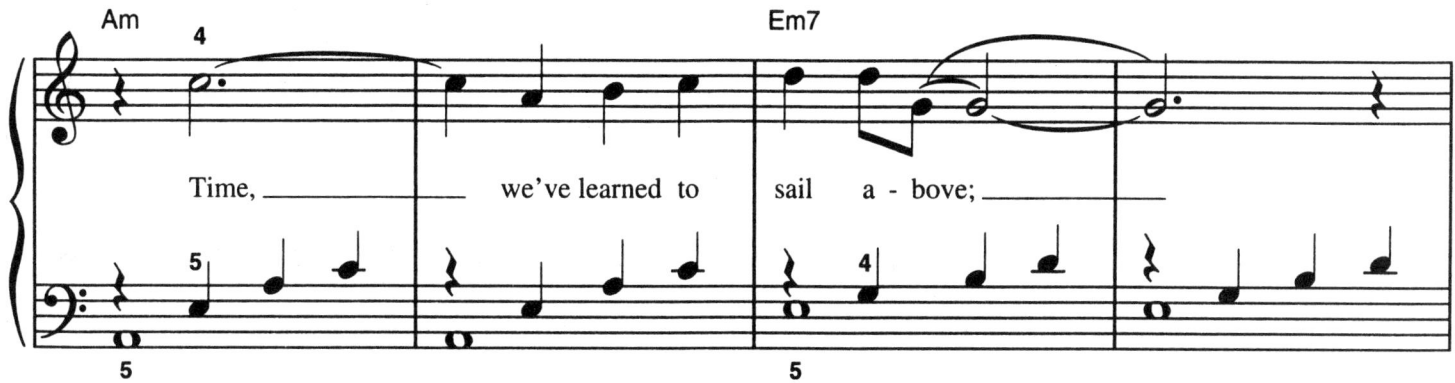
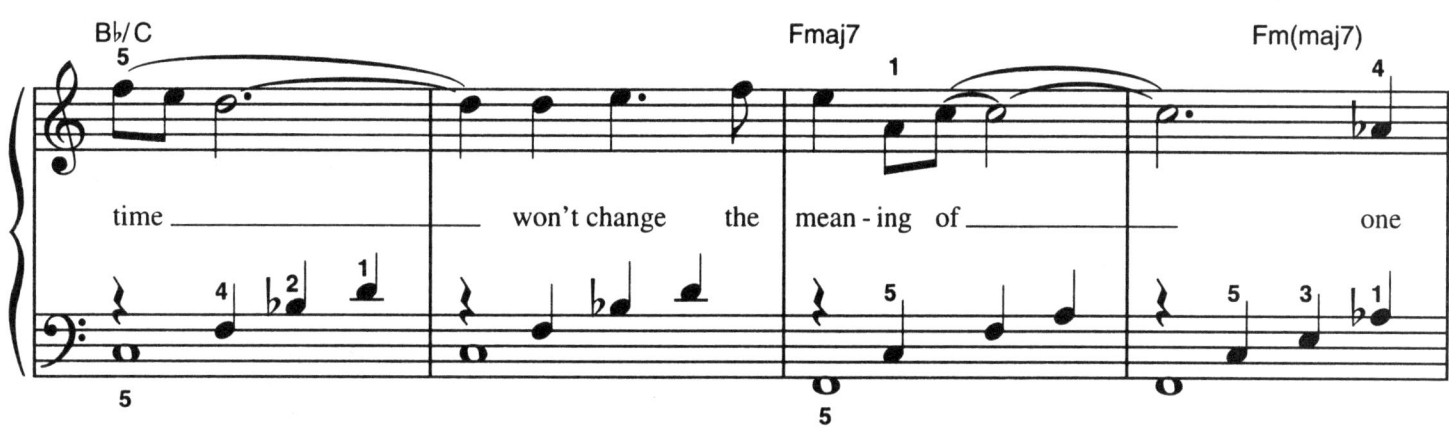

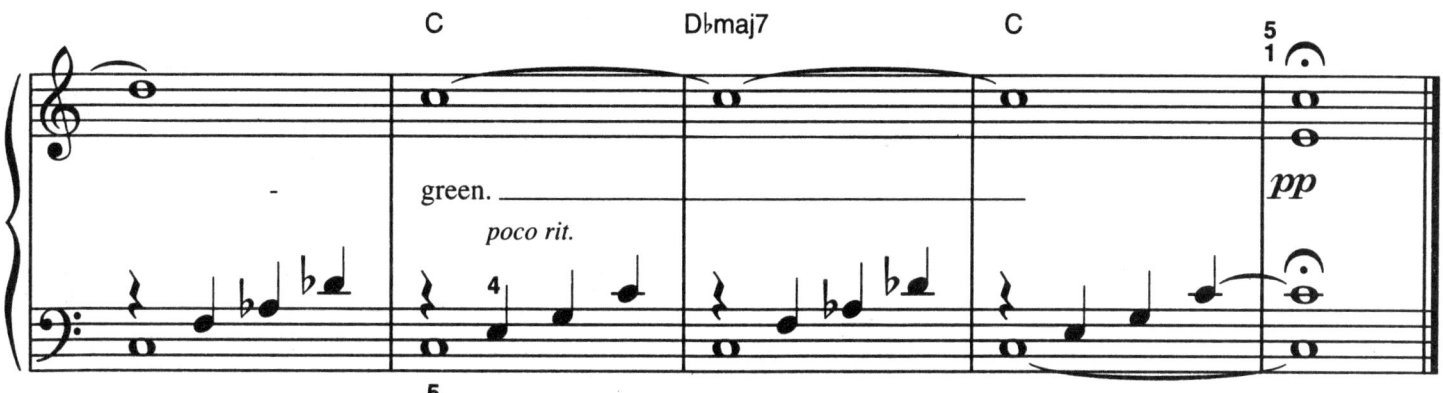

LITTLE BOY LOST
(Pieces of Dreams)

Arranged by
JOHN BRIMHALL

Lyrics by ALAN and MARILYN BERGMAN
Music by MICHEL LEGRAND

Lit-tle Boy Lost ___ in search of Lit-tle Boy Found. ___ You go a-won-der-ing, wan-der-ing, stum-bl-ing, tum-bl-ing, round, round! When will you find ___ what's on the tip of your mind? ___

© 1970 UNITED ARTISTS MUSIC CO., INC.
All Rights Controlled by Emi U CATALOG INC. (Publishing)
and WARNER BROS. PUBLICATIONS U.S. INC. (Print)
All Rights Reserved

LAURA

Arranged by
JOHN BRIMHALL

Lyric by JOHNNY MERCER
Music by DAVID RAKSIN

LOVE IS A MANY-SPLENDORED THING

Arranged by JOHN BRIMHALL

Lyrics by PAUL FRANCIS WEBSTER
Music by SAMMY FAIN

OVER THE RAINBOW

Arranged by
JOHN BRIMHALL

Lyric by E. Y. HARBURG
Music by HAROLD ARLEN

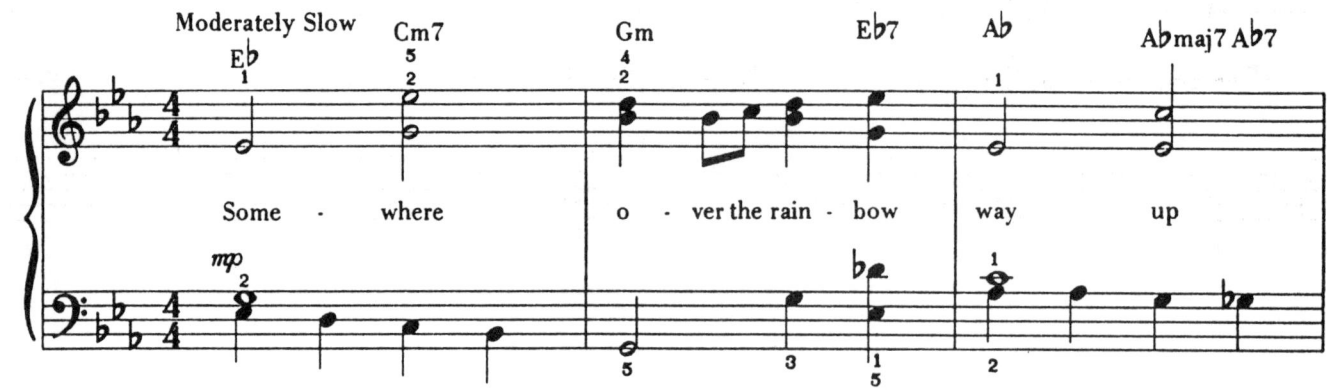
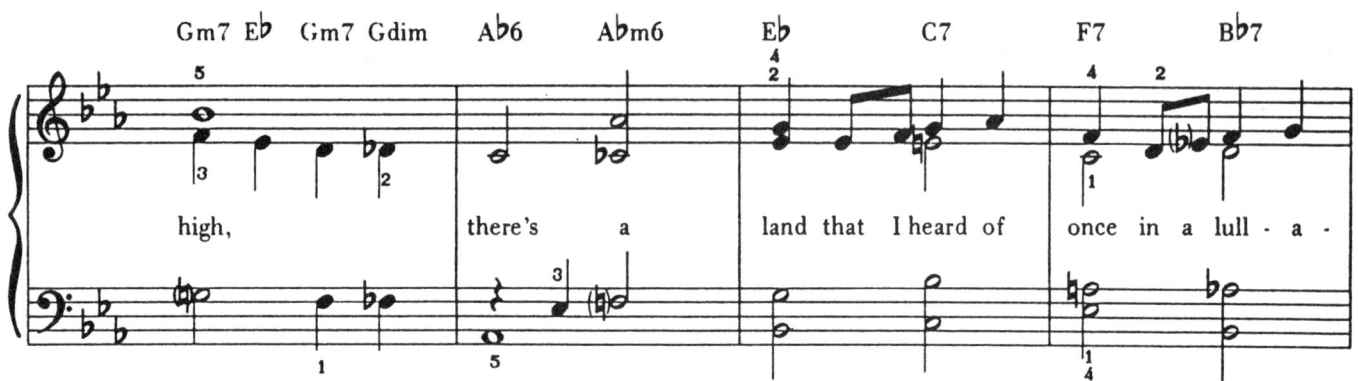
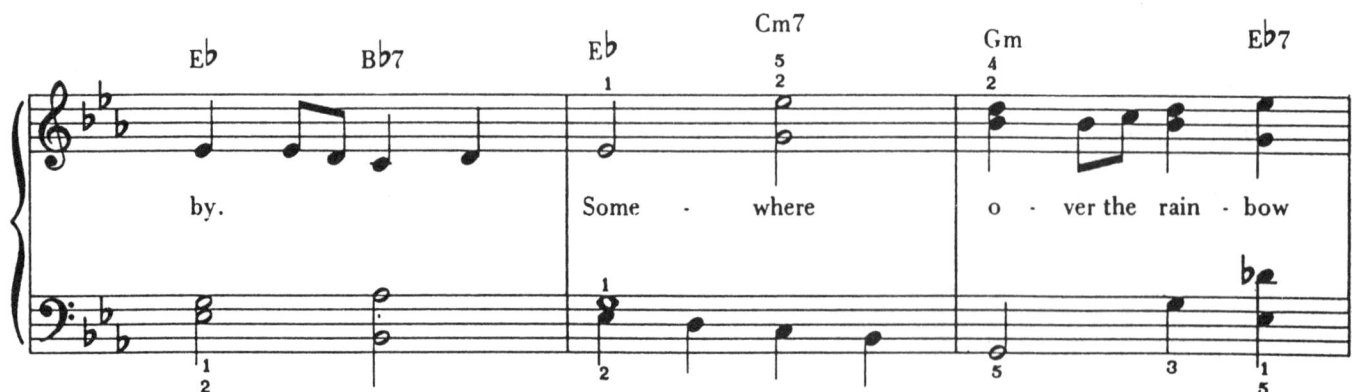
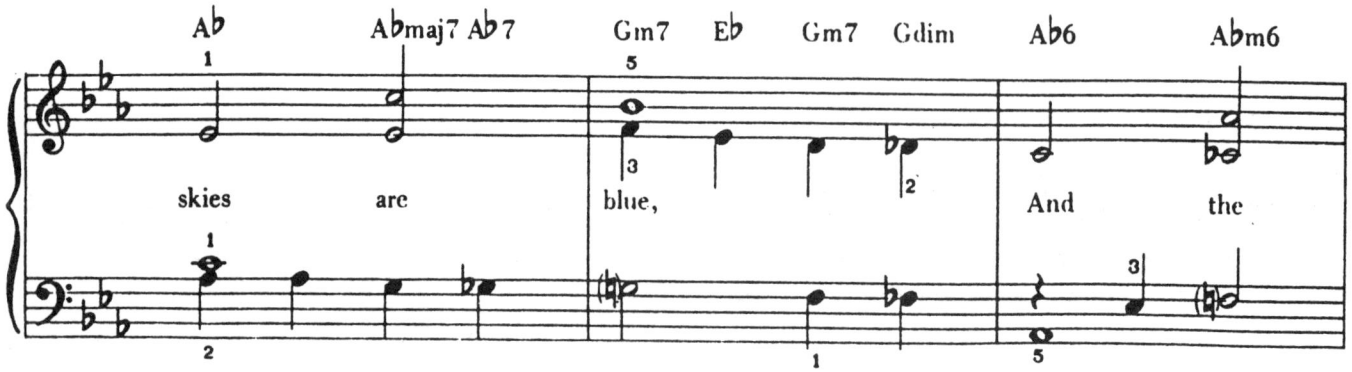

Over the Rainbow - 3 - 1

© 1938 (Renewed 1965) METRO-GOLDWYN-MAYER INC.
© 1939 (Renewed 1966) EMI FEIST CATALOG INC.
Rights throughout the World Controlled by EMI FEIST CATALOG INC. (Publishing) and WARNER BROS. PUBLICATIONS U.S. INC. (Print)
All Rights Reserved

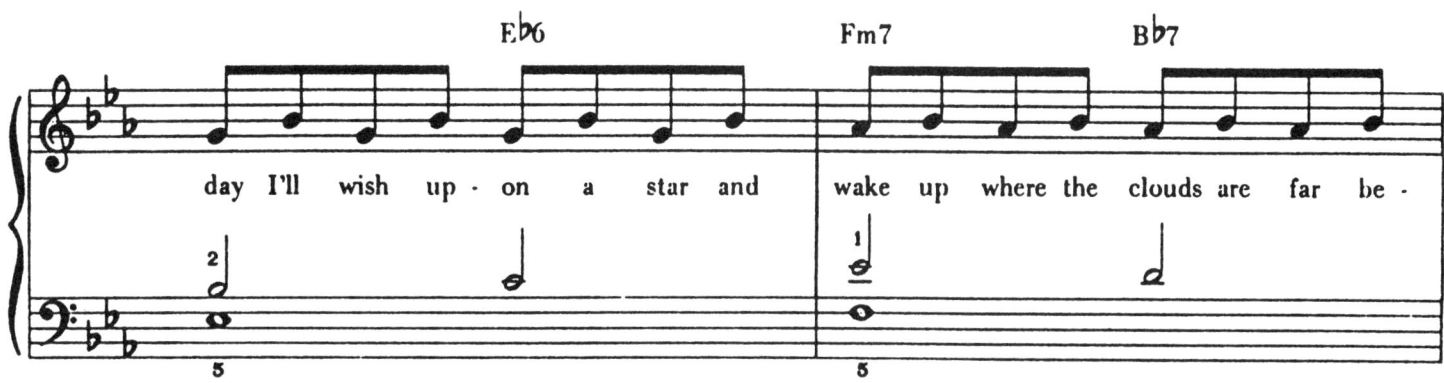
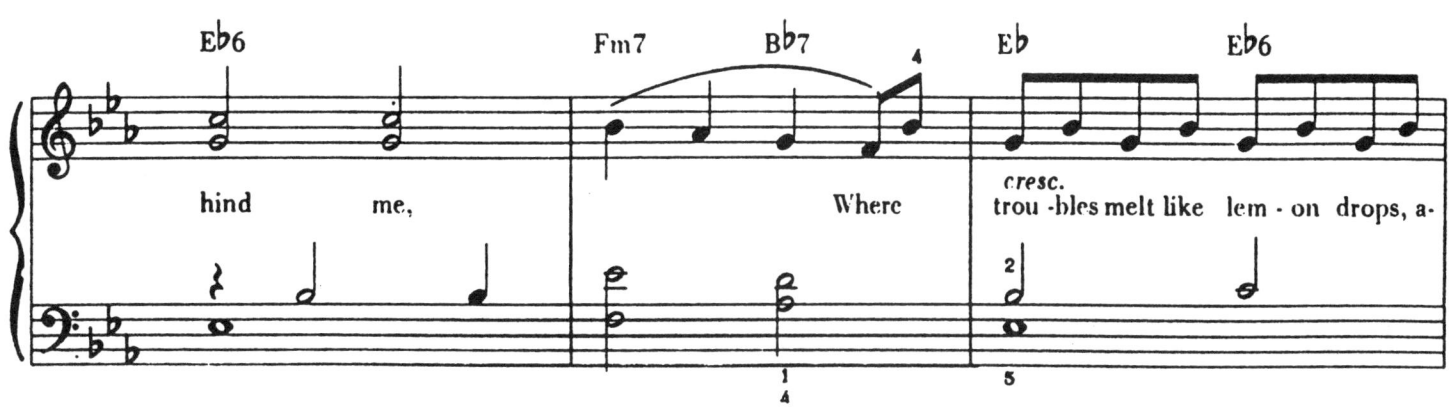
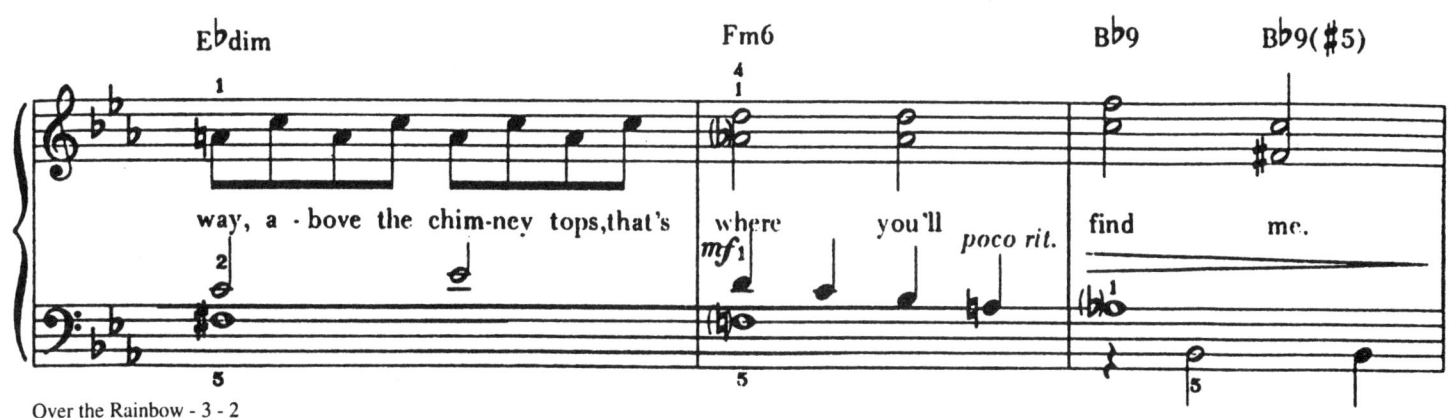

SECRET LOVE

Arranged by JOHN BRIMHALL

Words by PAUL FRANCIS WEBSTER
Music by SAMMY FAIN

Secret Love - 3 - 1

© 1953 WARNER BROS. INC. (Renewed)
This Arrangement © 1996 WARNER BROS. INC.
All Rights Reserved

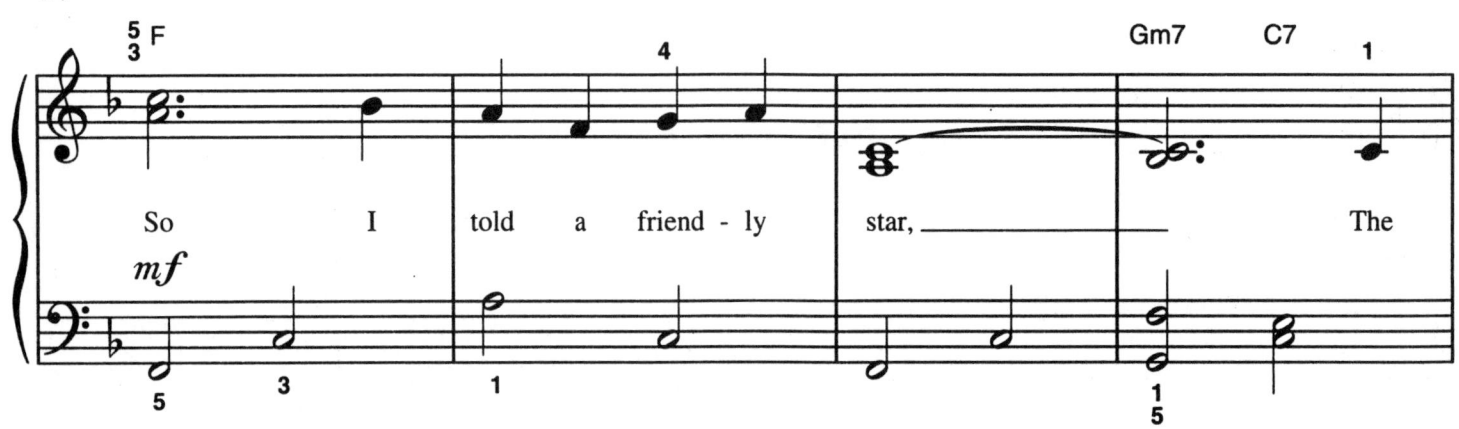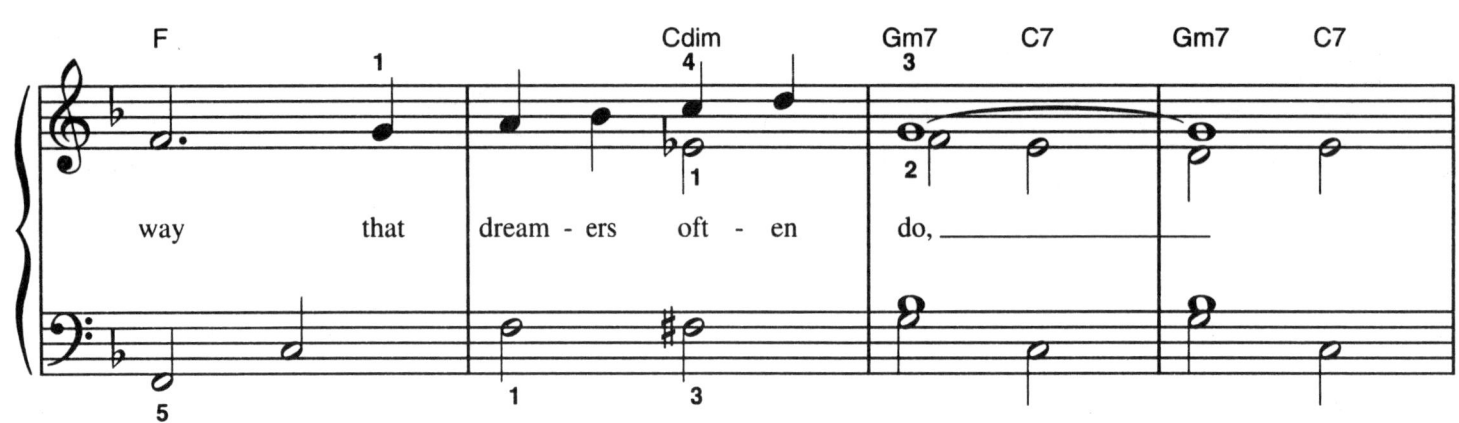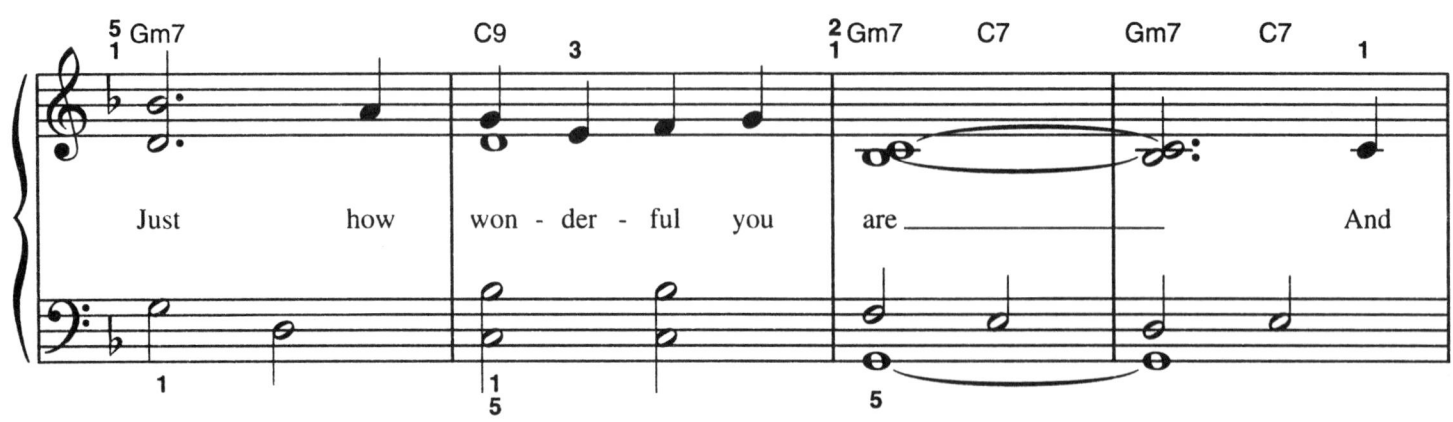

35

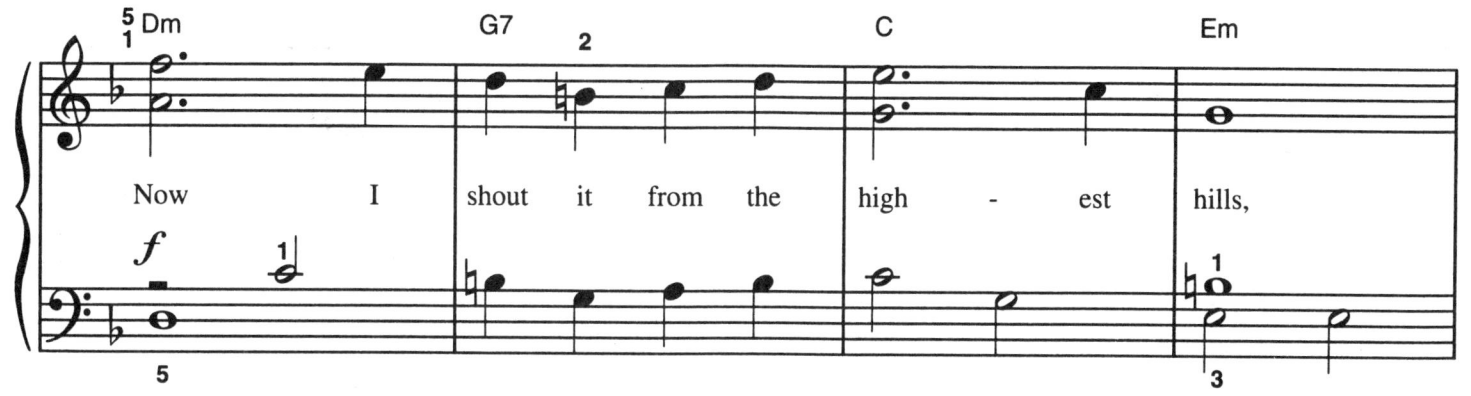
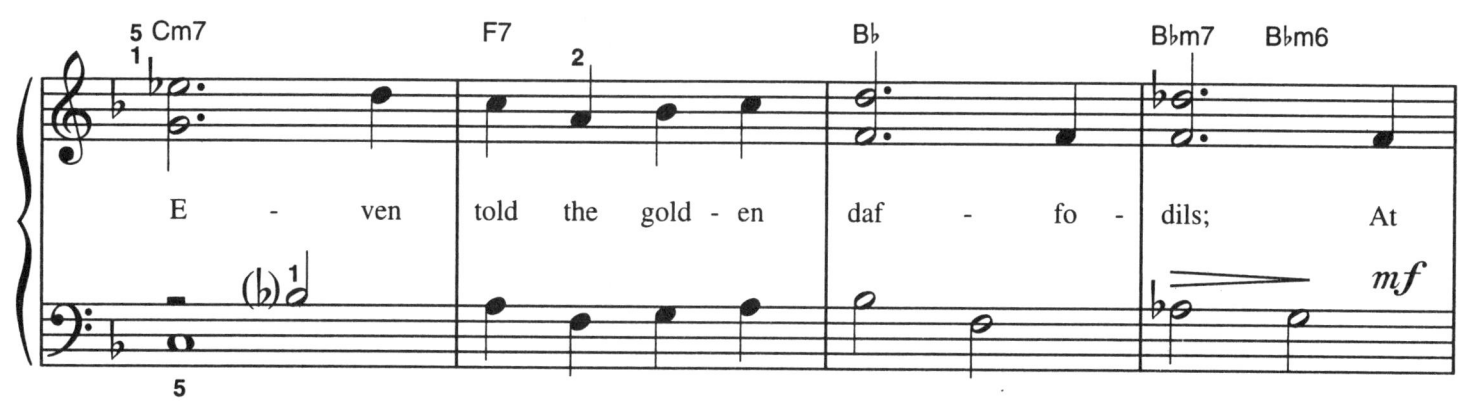
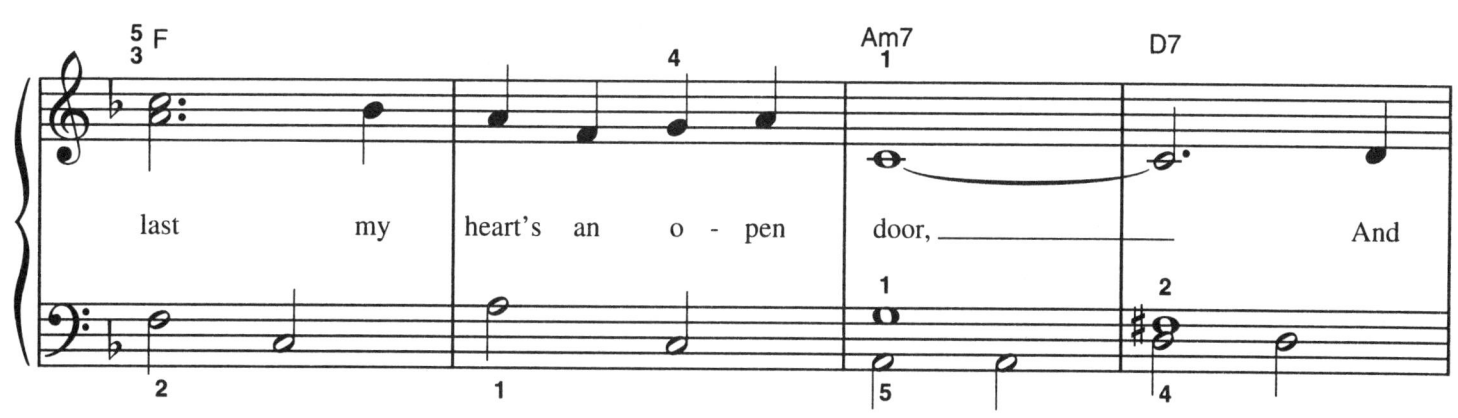
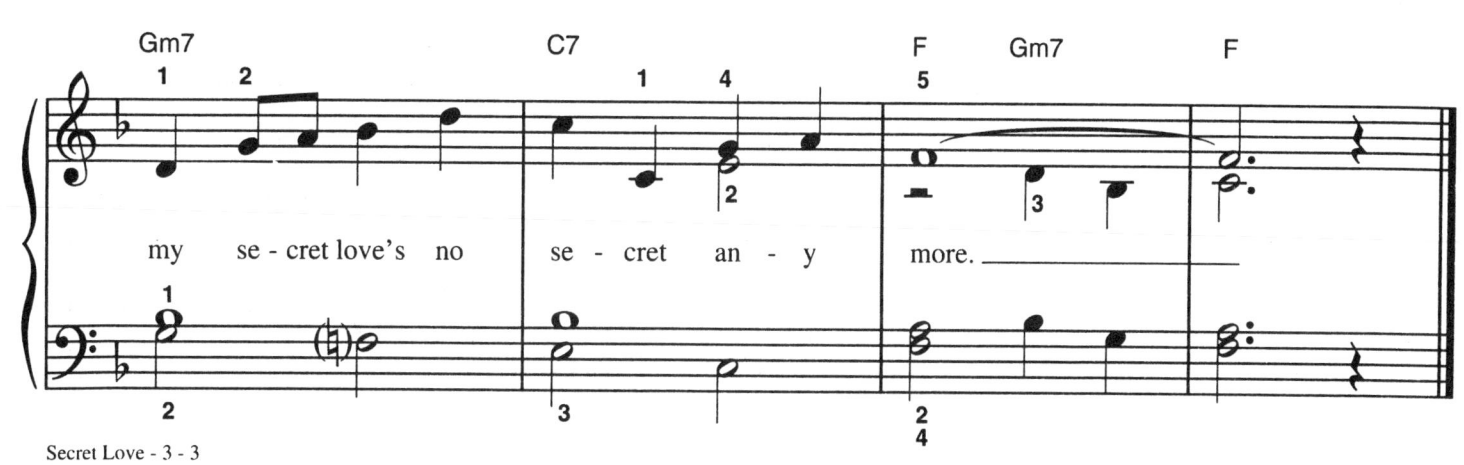

Secret Love - 3 - 3

THE SHADOW OF YOUR SMILE

(Love Theme from "The Sandpiper")

Arranged by
JOHN BRIMHALL

Words by PAUL FRANCIS WEBSTER
Music by JOHNNY MANDEL

THREE COINS IN THE FOUNTAIN

Arranged by
JOHN BRIMHALL

Words by SAMMY CAHN
Music by JULE STYNE

Three coins in the foun-tain, each one seek-ing hap-pi-ness
Three hearts in the foun-tain, each heart long-ing for its home,

Thrown by three hope-ful lov-ers.
There they lie in the foun-tain,

Which one will the foun-tain bless?
Some-where in the heart of Rome.

Which one will the foun-tain bless? Which one will the foun-tain

Three Coins in the Fountain - 2 - 1

© 1954 EMI Robbins Catalog Inc.
© Renewed 1982 CAHN MUSIC COMPANY and PRODUCERS MUSIC PUB. CO., INC.
All Rights on behalf of CAHN MUSIC COMPANY Administered by WB MUSIC CORP.
All Rights on behalf of PRODUCERS MUSIC PUB. CO., INC. Administered by CHAPPELL & CO.
All Rights Reserved

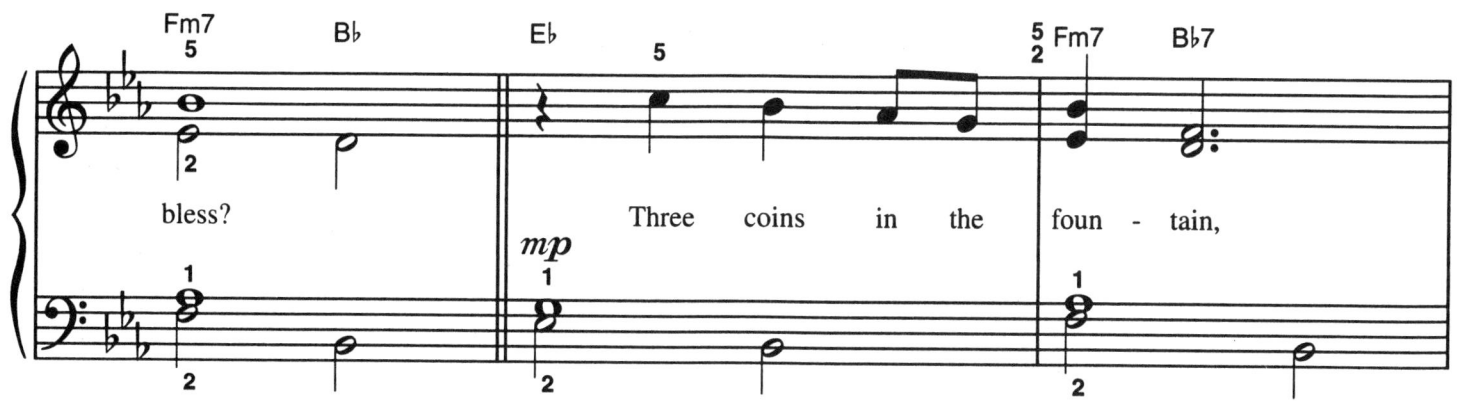
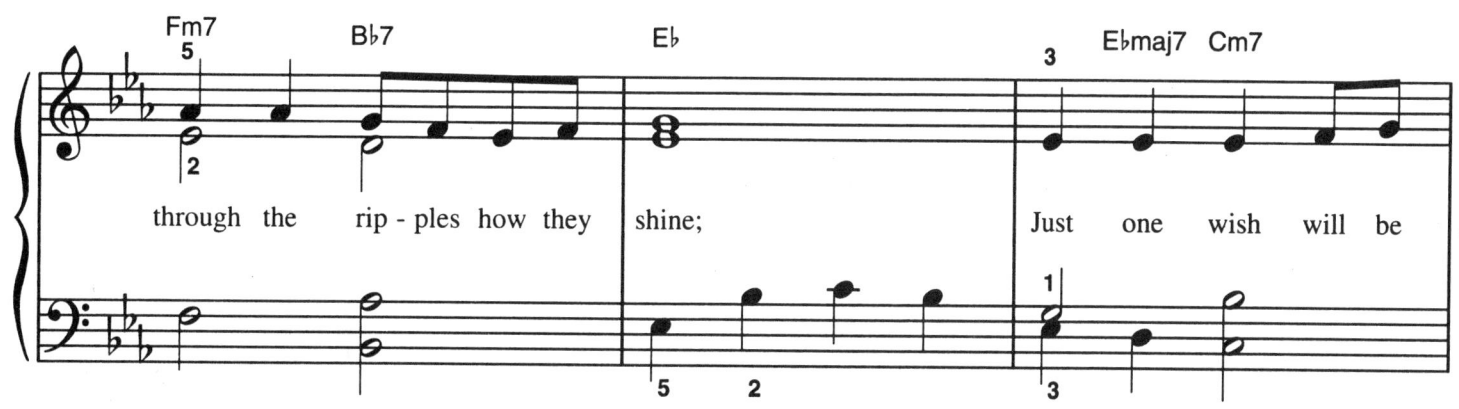

WHATEVER WILL BE, WILL BE
(Que Sera, Sera)

Arranged by
JOHN BRIMHALL

Words and Music by
JAY LIVINGSTON and RAY EVANS

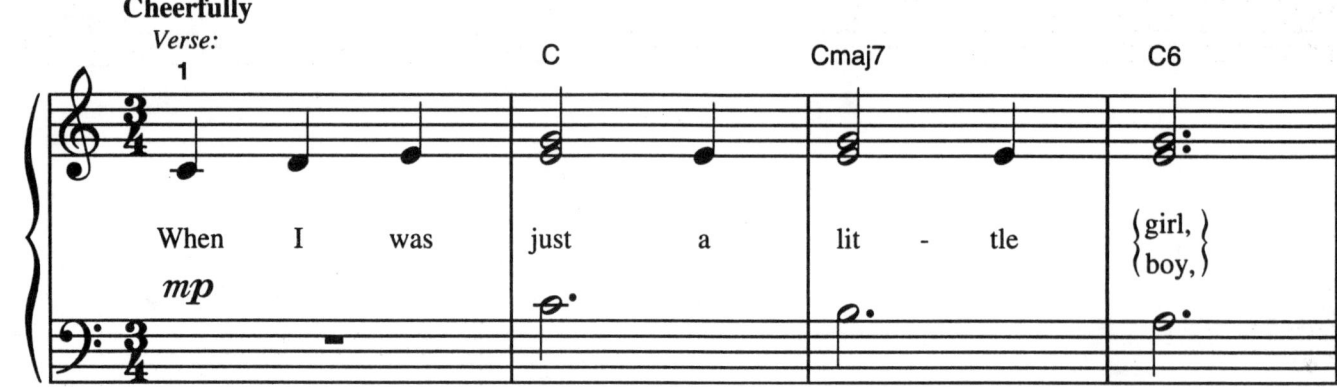

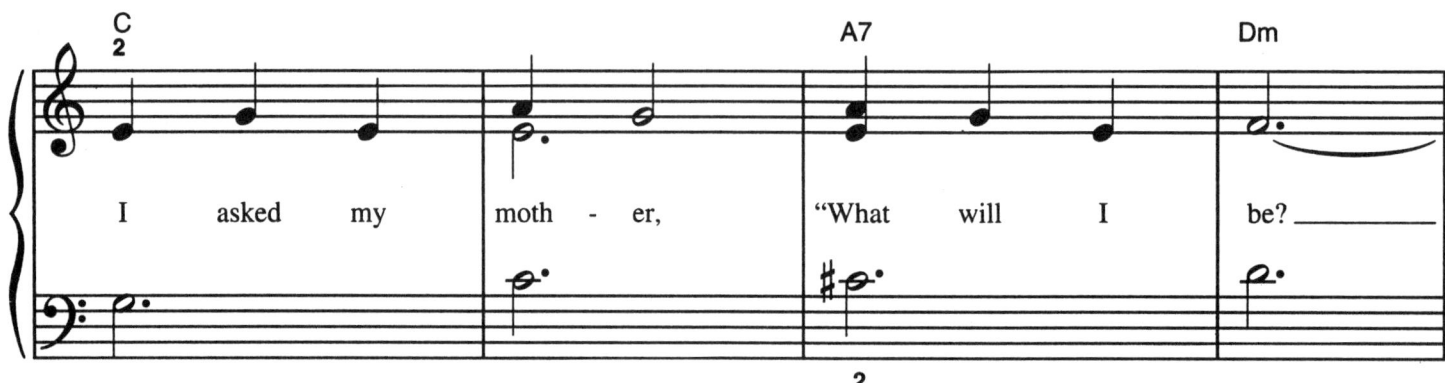

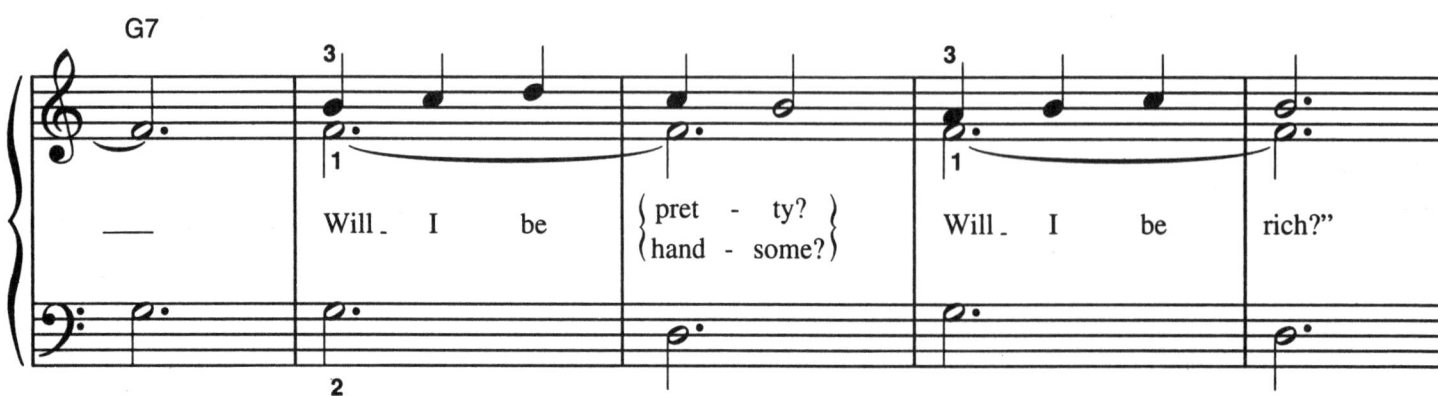

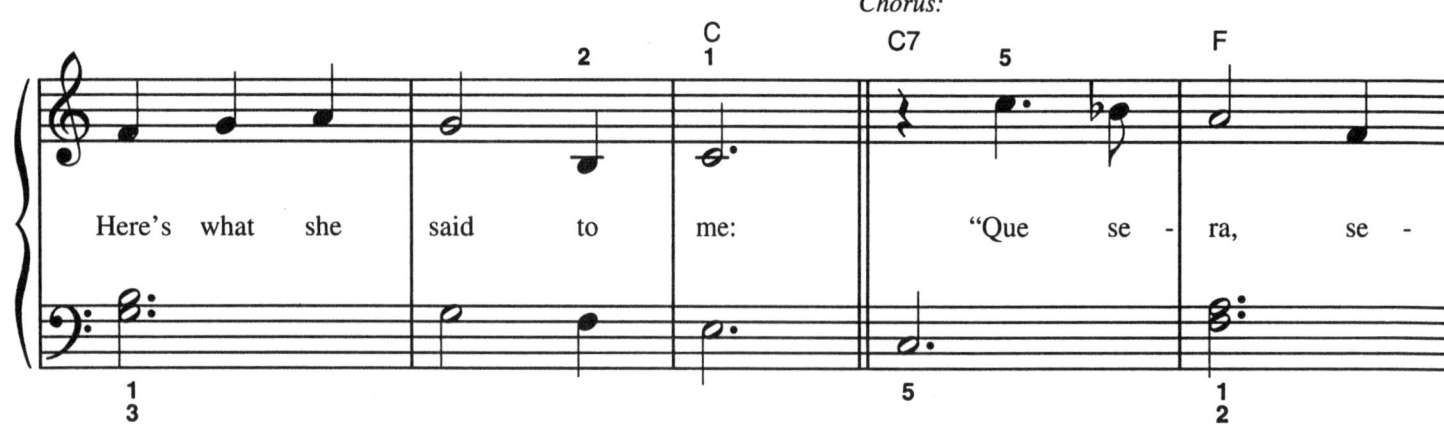

© 1955 by St. Angelo Music and Jay Livingston Music
Copyright Renewed
All Rights for St. Angelo Music Controlled and Administered by Universal - MCA Music Publishing,
A Division of Universal Studios, Inc.
All Rights Reserved

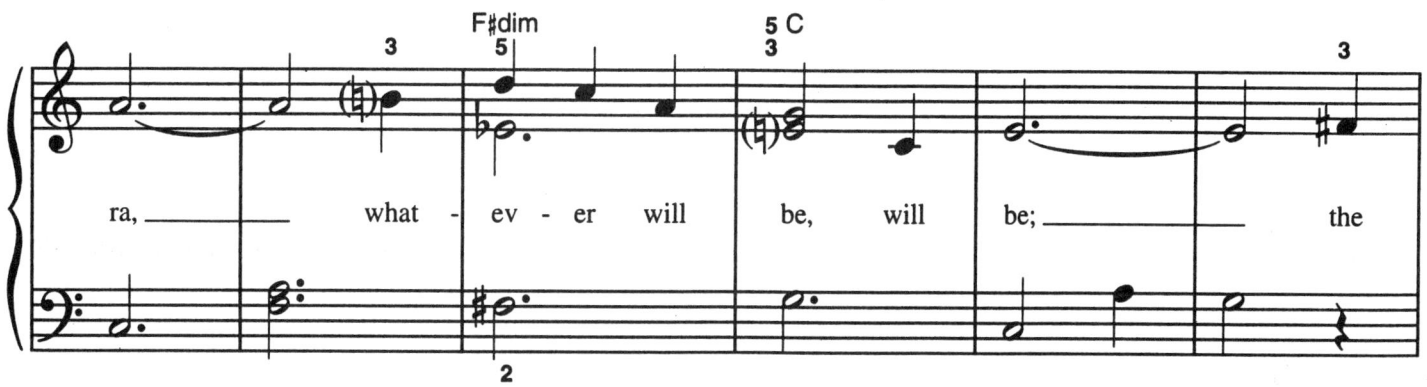
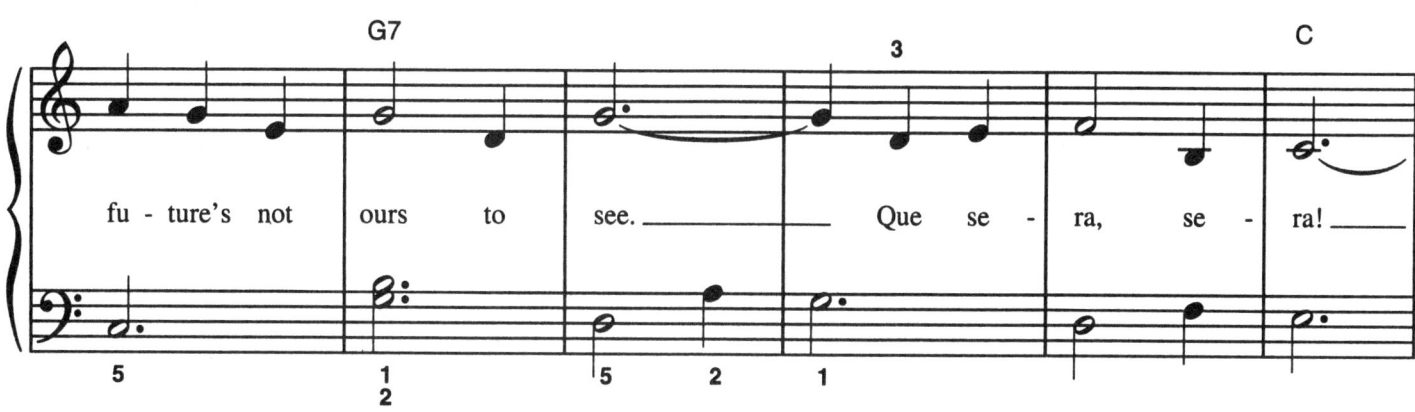
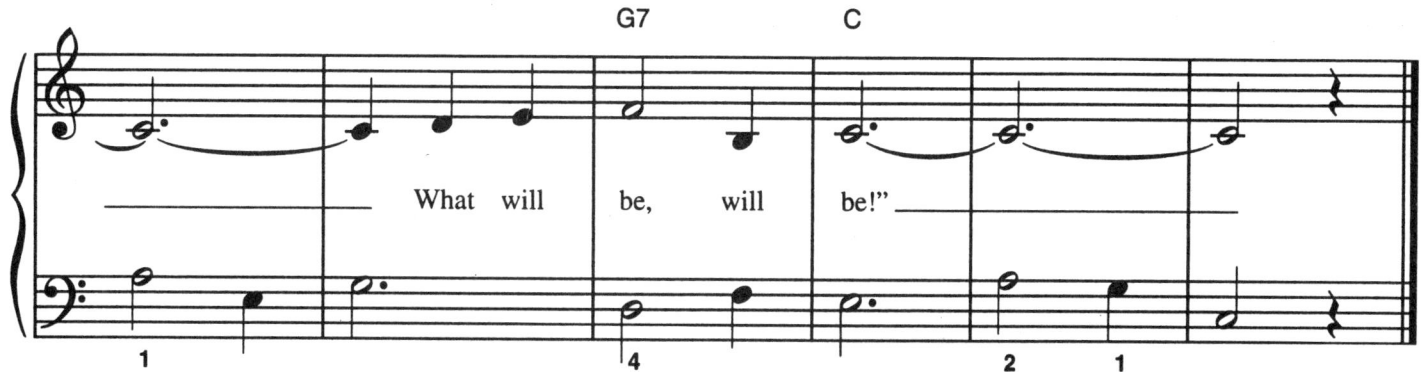

Additional Verses:

2. When I was just just a child in school,
   I asked my teacher, "What should I try?
   Should I paint pictures? Should I sing songs?"
   This was her wise reply:
   Chorus:

3. When I grew up and fell in love,
   I asked my { lover, / sweetheart, } "What lies ahead?
   Will we have rainbows day after day?"
   Here's what my { lover / sweetheart } said:
   Chorus:

4. Now I have children of my own,
   They ask their { mother, / father, } "What will I be?
   Will I be { pretty? / handsome? } Will I be rich?"
   I tell them tenderly:
   Chorus:

YOUNG AT HEART

Words by CAROLYN LEIGH
Arranged by JOHN BRIMHALL

Music by JOHNNY RICHARDS

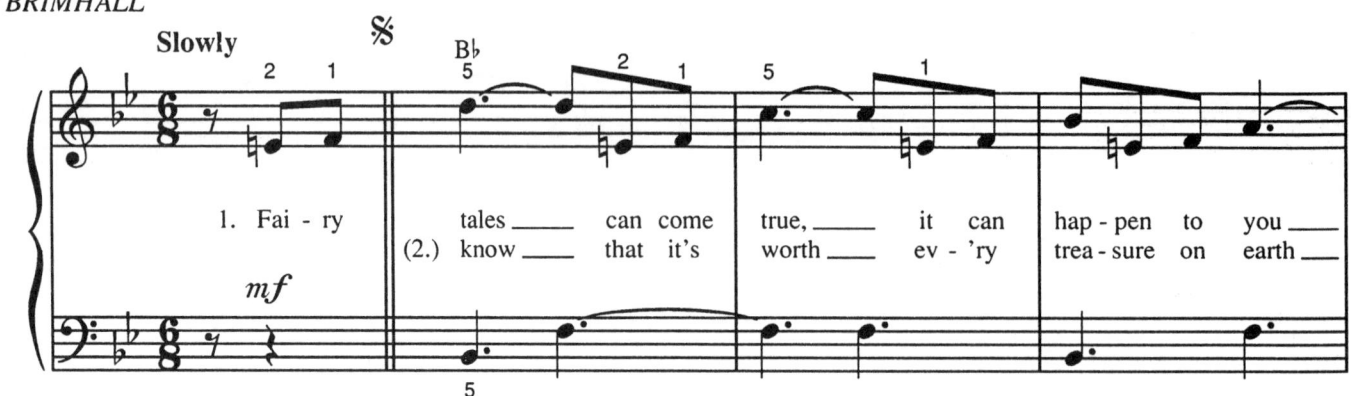

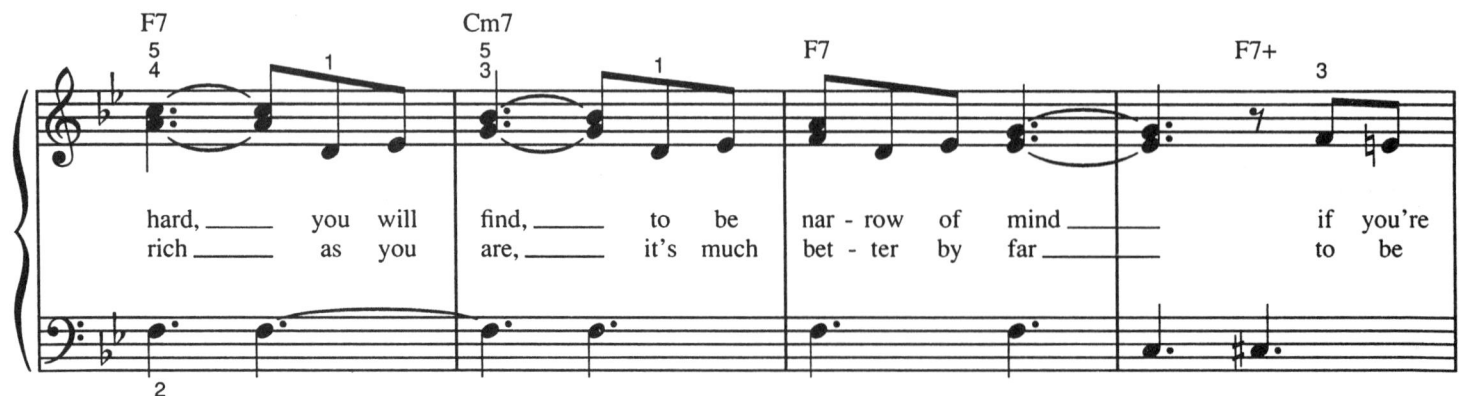

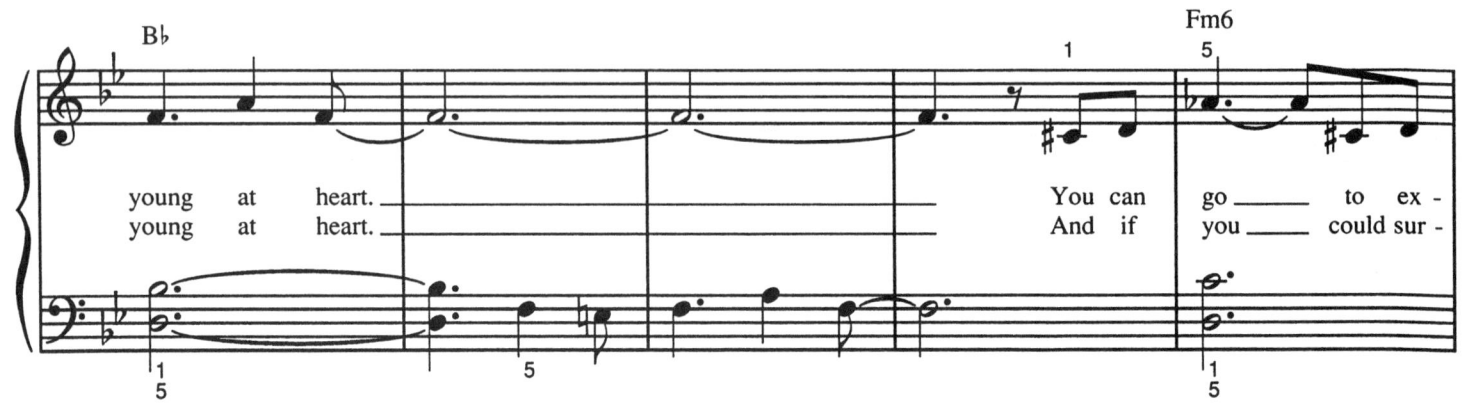

© 1954 CHERIO CORPORATION
© Renewed 1982 and Assigned to CAROLYN LEIGH and CHERIO CORPORATION
All Rights Reserved

THE SUMMER KNOWS
(Theme from "Summer of '42")

Arranged by JOHN BRIMHALL

Lyrics by MARILYN and ALAN BERGMAN
Music by MICHEL LEGRAND

© 1971 WB MUSIC CORP.
This Arrangement © 1996 WB MUSIC CORP.
All Rights Reserved

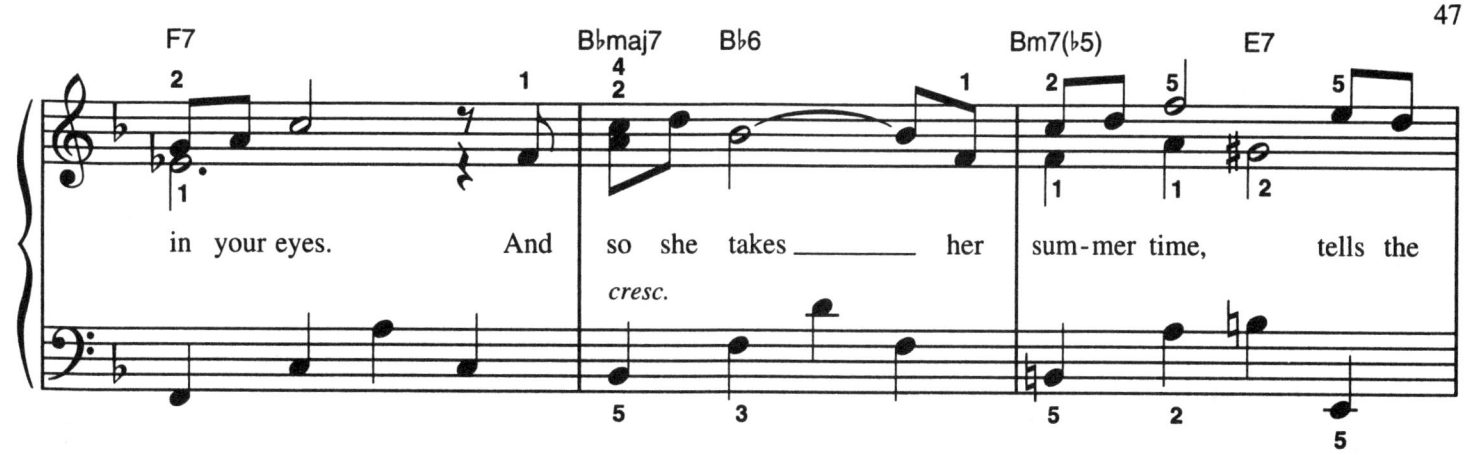
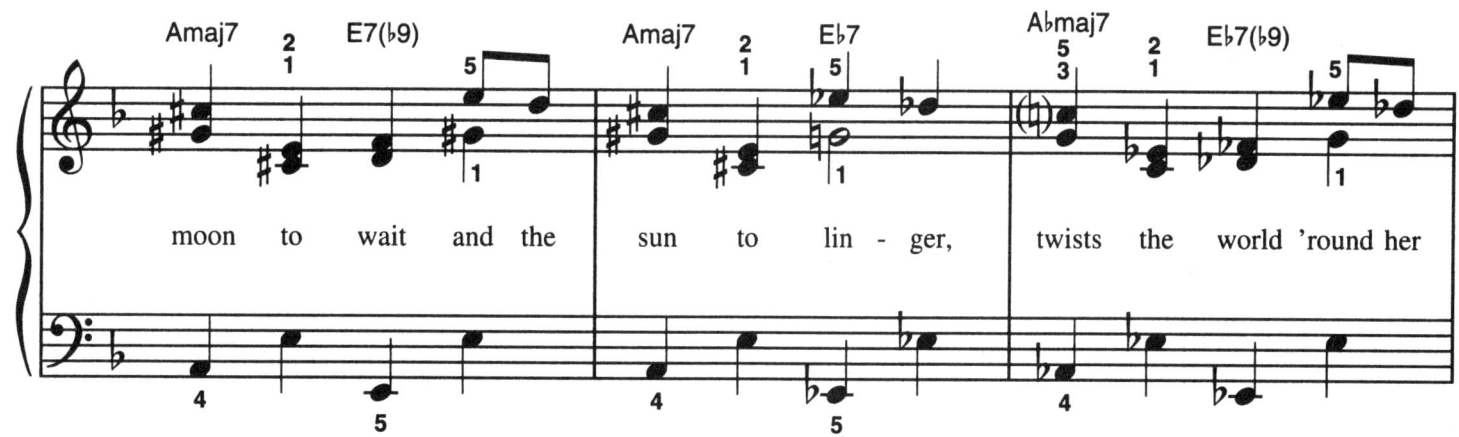

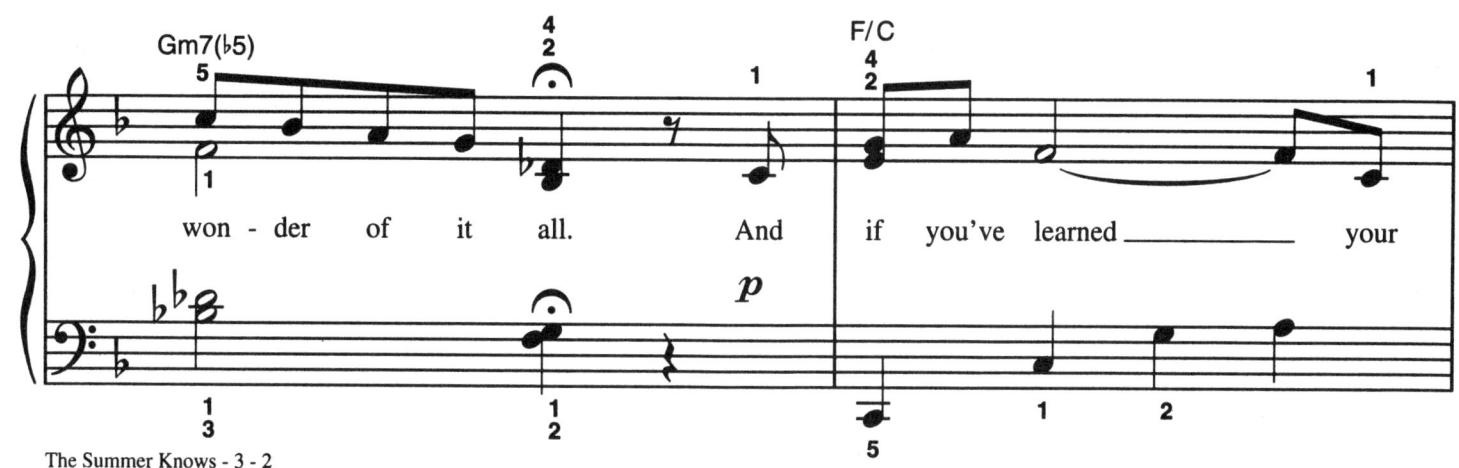

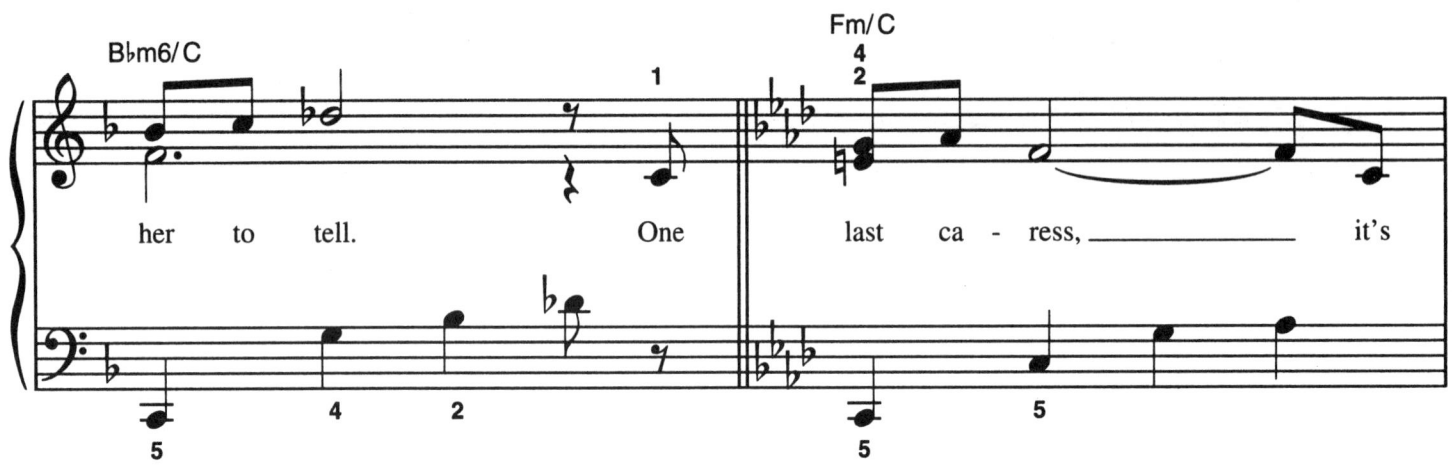
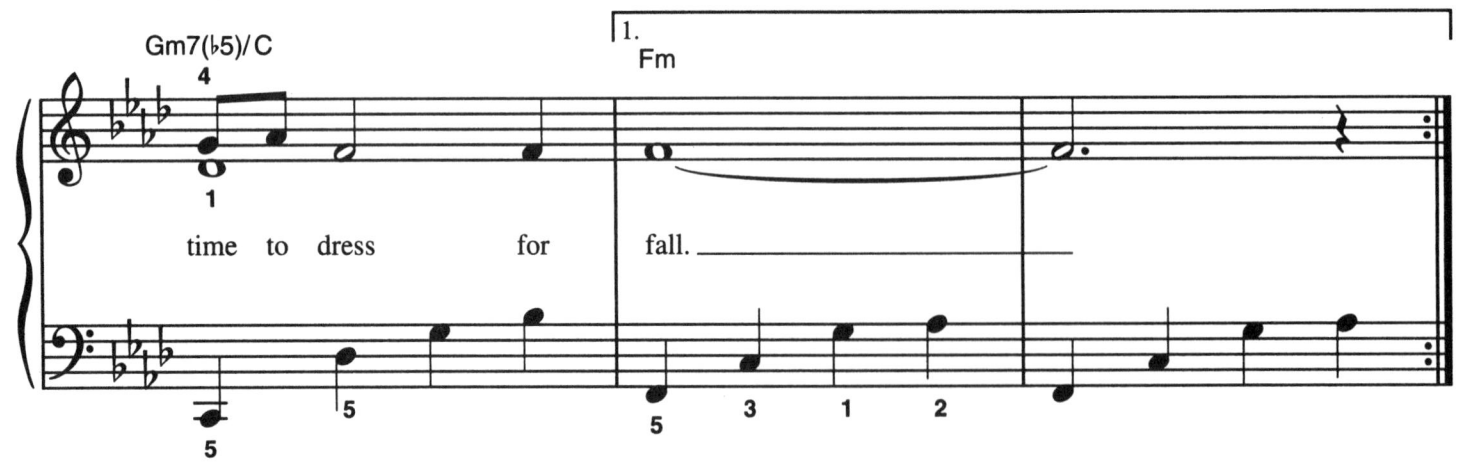
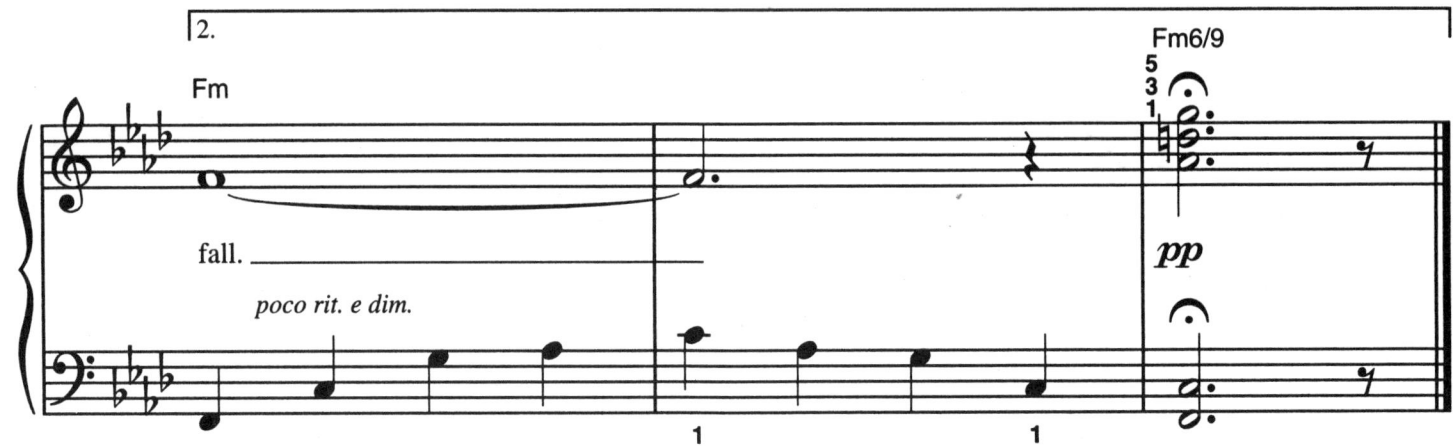